POTKIN AND STUBBS

THE HAUNTING OF PELIGAN CITY

SOPHIE
GREEN

Illustrated by
K. J. Mountford

Piccadilly
PRESS

First published in Great Britain in 2019 by
PICCADILLY PRESS
80–81 Wimpole St, London W1G 9RE
www.piccadillypress.co.uk

A CIP catalogue record for this book is available from the British
Library.

ISBN: 978-1-84812-763-0
also available as an ebook

1

Typeset by Palimpsest Book Production Limited,
Falkirk, Stirlingshire

Printed and bound in Great Britain by Clays Ltd, Elcograf S.p.A.

Piccadilly Press is an imprint of Bonnier Books UK
www.bonnierbooks.co.uk

To all those who keep the library doors open

Chapter 1

Alias Stellar Darke

It was mid-afternoon and snow was spiralling through the November sky, pure and white as it passed the street lamps, wet and grey as it touched the pavements of Peligan City. It was the kind of snow that made the air look grainy, ghosting out the tower blocks and the industrial chimneys on the horizon.

A small figure stood out against the gloom: Lil Potkin, woollen earmuffs nestled over her cup-handle ears and a thin scarf tucked into her bright yellow raincoat. Lil was perched on the back of a frosty wooden bench, in front of the Limelight Picture House on the corner of Spooner Row and Bead Street. Snow dusted her hair, gathered in her hood and slowly soaked its way through the leather of her boots.

On the seat below sat Nedly Stubbs, her friend and fellow investigator. Snow didn't land on him at all, because Nedly was a ghost. Thin, stooped and wearing nothing but a frayed grey sweatshirt, worn jeans and battered trainers, Nedly wasn't visible to anyone but Lil, although people felt his presence all the same: a whisper at the back of their neck, an icy spot to be avoided – something they might call *a bad case of the creeps*.

Nedly had been killed while trying to save a young man called Leonard Owl from the clutches of the evil genius Cornelius Gallows. Gallows, after faking his own death, had laid low for a decade, perfecting his macabre experimental procedure for capturing a ghost and binding it to his will. But on the night of his first attempt, unbeknownst to Gallows, two ghosts, not one,

were forged. One was Leonard's ghost, whom Gallows bound and called Mr Glimmer. The second ghost was Nedly, who escaped to wander invisible, confused and alone until he found someone willing to take on his case and discover exactly what had happened to him and why.

Nedly had waited for a year in the Paradise Street All-Night Bus Station before he met Lil. Lil had persuaded Abe Mandrel, the former police detective turned private eye, to join forces, and together they had solved the mystery of Nedly's murder, thwarted Gallows' evil plans and rescued his treacherous partner in crime, the disgraced former mayor Ramon LeTeef, from Gallows' most terrifying ghostly creation, Mr Grip.

Now Gallows had vanished again, but Lil was sure of one thing; he wasn't finished with Peligan City yet.

Across from where she and Nedly were sitting was an old warehouse with empty, snow-crusted windows and three steps leading to a bricked-up double doorway. Despite the cold, Lil had been staring at it without moving for over ten minutes. Her gaze was broken only by the occasional car splattering through the puddles of melted slush, or the odd passer-by hurrying along the pavement, eyes squinting against the snow, with their hat pulled down and their scarf wound high.

'I don't get it,' she murmured. 'Delilah's always there, that doorway is her home – it has been for years and now . . . Where is *she* and *who* is that guy in her spot?'

The man in question was lying inside a blue-and-orange sleeping bag in the midst of a carefully constructed den of old crates and flattened cardboard. He looked like an old brown moth emerging from a brightly coloured chrysalis. A trapper hat was pulled low over his eyes and his head was flopped back, mouth slightly open.

'Why don't you ask him?' said Nedly.

Lil bit her lip. 'I will. I just want to stake him out a bit before I go in. Now that I've had an article printed in the *Klaxon* I've got to keep a low profile.'

Nedly nodded soberly. 'Maybe you should get a less conspicuous coat?'

'This is my signature yellow mac. I can't just stop wearing it. *That* would look suspicious.'

The mac bore the scars of Lil's previous escapades: the left-hand sleeve was melted slightly and black soot had ingrained itself in the fabric when she had tried to rescue Abe Mandrel from his burning apartment; the stitching round the hood was loose where she had been grappled in a headlock by the ex-mayor of Peligan City's bodyguard; and there were puncture marks on both wristbands where a specially adapted crochet hook had tried to loosen the ropes that bound her hands when she was taken prisoner by Gallows in an abandoned asylum.

It had seen better days but it had character.

She pulled out a pencil that she had lodged in her hair and chewed on the end of it thoughtfully. She had wanted to keep it tucked behind her ear like her hero, the enigmatic investigative reporter A. J. McNair used to, but she didn't have the right kind of ears. Lil was also teaching herself to twiddle a pencil casually between her fingers like a baton. It was early days but it looked pretty good when she got it right.

McNair had been the chief journalist for the *Chronicle*, Peligan City's former newspaper. Legend had it that he had been killed while pursuing a political corruption story. The next day City Hall shut the *Chronicle* down and founded the *Herald* in its stead, and that was the last anyone in Peligan knew of the free press. Now the only place the real news was reported was in the *Klaxon*, an underground gazette written by a handful of anonymous reporters and circulated inside flyers for a non-existent restaurant, the Black Pug Eatery.

For as long as she could remember it had been Lil's dream to write for the *Klaxon*, but an undercover reporter with the alias Randall Collar had beaten her to the corruption scoop about Ramon LeTeef. Lil didn't mind as much as she thought she would; although they had never met, she admired Collar, and often dreamt that if she could get her hands on another really big political story, maybe they could work on it together. In fact, Lil had a fistful of dreams about the kind of reporter she'd like to become and she held on to them tightly. Now that she'd had her first article published – a half-page profile on Delilah Joan, a nightclub singer who had fallen on hard times and was usually found sleeping in the doorway opposite – Lil was sure her dreams were lined up to become a reality; behind the aroma of exhaust fumes and rubbish bins that hung in every street, she could sense a story lurking. She could almost smell the newsprint in the air.

'Well,' said Nedly, clearing his throat meaningfully, 'while we're waiting I want to show you something.'

Lil dragged her gaze away from the doorway. 'Go on then. I'm all eyes.'

He gulped. 'OK. Check this out.' He swivelled to face the Limelight Picture House, now showing a double bill of *Time is a Deadly Vice* and *The Night is Smoke and Shadows*.

The edge of the billboard was studded with light bulbs; Nedly narrowed his eyes at them, wriggled his shoulders and took a deep breath.

One of the bulbs dimmed, grew brighter, and dimmed again. Lil waited

'That's it?' she said eventually. Nedly's face fell.

'I'm actually controlling it!' he protested.

'Nedly. I thought you were going to be working on some serious moves. How long did it take you to learn that one?'

'Just a few weeks, but I've been working on something else at the same time so . . .'

'Weeks! You're supposed to be learning useful stuff like how to bend iron bars with your mind, or –'

'Are you talking to me?' An old woman in a corduroy cap and thick plastic glasses had stopped in front of the bench and was looking at Lil with alarm.

'No, sorry, I was just thinking out loud.' The edges of Lil's ears glowed scarlet. She waited for the woman to pass and then continued in a whisper, 'Or picking locks with your invisible fingers. Nedly, Gallows is still at large!'

'But you said learning to control electricity would be something worth knowing.'

Lil avoided Nedly's hurt look. She jumped down from the bench. 'It's just not the kind of thing I meant when I said "learn some combat skills". Gallows could strike at any minute!' She huffed as she jumped down from the bench and then skidded her way across the road to the man in the sleeping bag.

Lil leant across to give him a gentle prod and whispered, 'Hey, mister.'

He opened his eyes like his lids were spring-loaded. 'So you finally decided to come over?'

Lil nearly jumped out of her skin. 'I thought you were asleep!'

He tutted. 'I didn't even have my eyes properly closed. I was just keeping very still and there's no law against that.'

'I never said there was.' Lil tucked her hair behind her ears and then untucked it again. 'I just wanted to ask you something. You see, I'm looking for a woman called Delilah. She's always here . . . and now she's not.'

'And I am.' He let his eyelids droop and then flickered them open again. 'This is one of the best pitches in Peligan City – you know why? Down there is a furnace.' He jabbed a thumb over his shoulder, past the bricked-up doorway behind him. 'Keeps the cold out, day and night. Keeps me warm. Kept Delilah warm too for as long as she wanted it. But she didn't want it any more, so now it's mine.' He snuggled down into his bag and pulled the drawstring opening up to his chin. 'What is it to you?'

'Well, this investigative reporter wrote a profile of her and it got published in the *Klaxon*, which is this underground news pamphlet –'

'I know it.'

'Right.' Lil beamed. 'So you'll know it's a pretty big deal and I just thought she might like to see it.' She thumbed the piece of newsprint in her pocket that she had been carrying around with her ever since she'd been published. 'Maybe you'd like to read it yourself?'

Lil looked furtively over her shoulder and then took a step forward into the shelter of the doorway. The man was right; it was warmer in there. She held the news pamphlet out until his fingers emerged from the bag like a hermit crab from its shell and took hold of it.

He held the paper right up to his eyes and peered closely and then handed it back. 'Seen it already.'

'You have?' Lil had to work hard to keep the smile off her face as she repocketed the pamphlet. 'Well, I expect you're wondering who the new reporter Stellar Darke is, then.' She tried twiddling the pencil but it flew out of her fingers and disappeared into the man's cardboard nest.

'Who?'

Lil bit back an eye-roll. 'The intrepid reporter who wrote the article. You see, Stellar Darke will be an alias – it's not her, or his, real name.'

'Uh-huh.' The man settled back and closed his eyes.

'So even if I knew who it was, which I don't,

obviously, I couldn't tell you. It would go against the reporter's code of conduct, or something like that. It literally could be anyone. You . . .'

One eye opened a crack and then shut again. 'It's not me,' he assured her.

'Me,' Lil said hopefully.

He chuckled. 'That's even more unlikely than it being me; you can't be any older than ten.'

Lil gritted her teeth; her ears were getting hot. 'I'm nearly thirteen and it could be me. But it isn't,' she added quickly. 'But it could be.'

The man pushed himself further down in the sleeping bag and tugged the brim of his hat. 'Whatever you say.'

She swallowed hard. 'It wasn't you I wanted to show it to anyway. Like I said, I'm looking for Delilah.'

He nodded without opening his eyes. 'All right. If she comes by, I'll tell her. What did you say your name was again?'

'I didn't,' said Lil, mentally punching the air at being able to put her latest move, the 'Cryptic

Eyebrow raise' into action. She held it for a few seconds hoping that the man would open his eyes in time to catch it. He didn't.

'Well, good luck, whoever you are. No one has seen her for days.'

'No one?' Lil let the Cryptic Eyebrow drop into a frown. 'So where is she?'

'Beats me. The same place as the others I suppose.'

A cold feeling squirmed in Lil's belly. The falling snow surged as the wind changed direction and blew icily against her cheek. She shivered.

'What others?'

But the man in the doorway didn't reply, his eyes stayed shut and the breath whistled out of his nose.

Across the road Nedly was making three of the bulbs round the billboard flash on and off in a sequence. A little kid in a bobble hat was standing under the marquee of the picture house, watching the display, wide-eyed.

As Lil drew near the bench Nedly turned to face her. His smile was radiant. 'Like I said, it's just something I've been working on.' The smile drooped when he saw her expression. 'What did he say?'

Lil shrugged. 'Delilah's not there. She's vanished.' She squinted up the road. 'Something doesn't feel right.'

Nedly followed the direction of her gaze, into the shadows that lurked in the alleyways that cut between the buildings opposite. 'You say that nearly every day.'

Lil gave him a look. 'One day I'm going to be right.'

She shivered and – *bang!* – one of the light bulbs exploded suddenly. Nedly's pale skin had turned china white.

Lil looked at the fragments of shattered glass winking in the slush. The little kid was shaking tearfully, a woman came out from the box office, put her arm round him and ushered him inside.

Without taking her eyes away Lil whispered to Nedly. 'You feel it too, don't you? The creeps.'

Nedly didn't reply. He stuffed his hands into the pockets of his jeans and kicked at a ridge of filthy snow with his toe, knocking a couple of flakes off the top but leaving it otherwise intact.

Across town an alarm bell had started ringing.

Chapter 2

Mr Dose

The wheels of the hospital trolley twisted and squealed as it was roughhoused out of the cell. Its cargo, an old grey-faced man with conspicuous front teeth, was bound loosely with leather straps round his sunken chest, but they weren't necessary; he was too frail to escape, even if he wanted to.

Vassal Hench, the man pushing the trolley, wore his small pork-pie hat on the slant, like a garnish, over his thick oily hair. It was completely at odds with the orderly's uniform that stretched uneasily over his hunched shoulders. As the trolley moved past the rows of metal cages, eyes watched from the darkness behind the bars, and the occasional whimper was stifled with trembling hands. Those taken on the shrieking trolley never returned and no one knew who would be next.

Well, almost no one.

At the end of a winding stone tunnel the trolley reached its grim destination in the deepest part of the building. The air was dank and black mildew bloomed along the walls, mirroring the sinister dark stains on the floor.

A metal machine, about the size of a shoebox, hummed menacingly in the background, sprouting a tangle of discs on wires like suckers. Hench wrangled the trolley towards it and then jumped as a thin man stepped out of the shadows before him.

'Trouble, Hench?' The speaker, Cornelius Gallows, wore a surgical mask and a long rubber apron over his doctor's coat. His deep-set eyes watched coldly from under his hairless brow.

'Quiet as a lamb, Dr Gallows,' Hench replied, shakily mopping his forehead with a red-spotted handkerchief.

Gallows' left eyelid twitched as he examined the man on the trolley. He fixed two adhesive discs on either side of the man's bony temples, and two on his chest. Then he held out a hand impatiently, clicking his fingers.

Hench passed him a poppet made from white flour-sacking sewn with heavy black thread and stuffed with straw. A face had been stitched on – crosses for eyes, a straight-stitch mouth – and tacked to the topknot where the cloth was gathered and fastened with string, was a tiny bell. Gallows placed the poppet across the man's chest, where it lay barely rising and falling with his shallow, wheezing breaths.

Gallows' fingertips quivered as he turned a dial on the machine. Electricity surged through the wires; the adhesive discs crackled and sparked. The old man's eyes snapped open, his body jerked and his mouth formed a scream that never sounded.

A sickly smell of burning fizzed in the air.

The old man lay there, no longer breathing. His eyes stared blankly. Gallows took out a stethoscope and held it against the corpse's chest. He listened for a minute and then nodded to himself.

The air grew cold and clammy. The emergency lamps buzzed and dimmed. Gallows looked at the thermometer on the wall.

'It's here,' he whispered. 'The one we will call "Mr Dose".'

Hench gave an involuntary shudder.

Gallows' colourless eyes observed him. 'I thought you would be used to this by now, Hench.' Then he plucked the poppet from the dead man and gave it a shake. The little bell tinkled softly.

'Here, boy,' he murmured, watching the mercury in the thermometer fall. *Tinkle tinkle.*

'Here, boy,' Hench repeated, smirking but only half-heartedly, because although he couldn't see Mr Dose, he knew he was there, a newly arrived presence full of brooding malice and dark thoughts, and it made his skin crawl.

By the time Lil and Nedly emerged from the Limelight Picture House the sky was blue and slightly luminous, but with the bruised look that the snow brought. They heard the metallic scrape of the grille being pulled down over the kiosk as soon as their feet hit the pavement. It wasn't even that late but things didn't seem to stay open like they used to.

A gust blew in and with a sudden rustling sound something pale flew out from the shadows. Lil stepped back out of its path but the discarded newspaper wrapped itself over her boot. She tried to kick it off but it clung on like a wet flannel. The cheap ink had already bled but she could just make out the headline from the previous day's edition of the *Herald*: 'Gordian Vows to Clean Up Peligan!' before it vanished into a grey smudge.

She looked at the rubbish bagged up on the

street corner, split and spilling its insides all over the pavement, and the tins and papers blowing with the wind. Maybe the streets were getting cleaner in the city centre; here in the old town they looked just the same as always. And alongside the grime and the disrepair an uneasy feeling had started to grow. It grated like a melody played off-key in a cheap piano bar. Things were out of tune. Lil could sense a story building, and if she was going to bag the scoop this time, she knew she had to get a clue before it broke.

They stopped at the corner to wait for a break in the slow procession of traffic. Taxi cabs with their headlights on cut streaks in the dark as they crawled by. Snow started to fall more heavily, the large flakes like feathers from exploded pillows.

Across the road a soft glow emanated from the Nite Jar Cafe; it was the sort of joint where the coffee was always hot and the juke box played nothing but jazz. Lil and Nedly headed towards it.

Inside, the coffee maker was blowing out steam that clung to the cold glass of the windows, and a few of the regulars were holed up in the red-leather booths, glad to be off the street for a few hours.

As soon as she stepped over the threshold all the snow that had landed on Lil began to melt and she raced to peel off her mac and unravel her scarf.

The waitress, in black slacks and a mint-green polo shirt with 'Nite Jar Cafe' embroidered on the pocket, took the mac and shook the snow out of it.

'You're early.'

'Hi, Velma!' Lil glanced admiringly at Velma's backcombed and smoothed cone-shaped hair-do. 'I was in town already so I thought maybe I'd just come straight over. Can I get my tea here again tonight?'

'Yoshi?' Velma called out to the short-order cook through the hatch. 'Can I get a cheese on toast for our young pot-washer here, please?'

'Coming up!' the voice called back.

'Yoshi?' Lil called. 'Can you make that with extra pickle?' She paused and then added causally, 'and why don't you throw a couple of olives on there too?'

Yoshi stuck his head round the kitchen door and smiled. His dark hair was sweated into points along his forehead and his 'Nite Jar Cafe' polo shirt was customised with greasy handprints. 'Olives on grilled cheese? You know, no one has asked for that since. . .' He and Velma exchanged a look. 'Well, a long time ago. Take a seat and I'll bring it over.'

Nedly snorted a 'Really?' as they made their way to the booth at the far end of the cafe.

'It's no big deal.' Lil sat down with her back to the counter.

'Didn't the intrepid reporter A. J. McNair used to have olives on his cheese on toast?'

Lil gave Nedly her trademark Penetrating Squint. 'Have you been reading my book?'

Nedly grinned. 'Just been practising turning the pages and happened to see that bit.'

'Maybe McNair and I have similar taste. Who knows.'

Lil rubbed a porthole in the steamed-up window. On the other side of the road the newsagent was changing the sodden newspaper on the A-board. She watched him slide the evening edition of the *Herald* into place. Its headline was: 'Fellgate Epidemic Killing Off Prisoners Saves Peligan City Thousands'.

'That's a pretty sour way to look at it.'

Lil could see Fellgate Prison, known to all as 'the Needle', from her house. It took the shape of a long, thin tower that broke the horizon, forever lit up by search beams that arced across the sky.

A few minutes later Yoshi came out with her food. 'So, you hear the news?'

Lil raised her eyebrows. 'Maybe, what gives?'

'The latest news, just happened. About Silverman, financial adviser over at Peligan Savings and Loans. Very big mystery, lots of intrigue.'

'What do you know?' Lil picked an olive from the molten cheese and casually popped it into her mouth. Her face stiffened as she got a taste of the unexpectedly briny pellet.

'Caretaker came in for a strong tea one hour ago; rumour is that Silverman fell off the roof of the building.' Lil choked on the olive as she tried to swallow it. Yoshi gave her a restorative thump on the back. 'He's dead.'

Chapter 3

These Pots Aren't Going
to Wash Themselves

'Silverman . . . dead? Was it . . . suicide?' Lil's voice was strained as she held another cough at bay.

'Caretaker thought maybe Silverman didn't jump,' said Yoshi. 'Maybe he was pushed.'

'But,' Velma added, joining them, 'the police who came in after to pick up their donuts for the evening shift said that he definitely did. He was all by himself up there.'

'Not what the caretaker said,' Yoshi countered.

Velma sighed and planted a frosted-pink lipstick kiss on Yoshi's cheek 'I don't expect we'll ever know what really happened.' She nodded at Lil's plate. 'Have you changed your mind about the olives?'

'No, I'm just saving them 'til last. They're my favourite bit.' Lil didn't even want to look at them.

Velma shrugged and she and Yoshi left them to it.

'I actually do like olives,' Nedly said and tried to pick one up. With a good deal of effort he floated it unsteadily above his head and then, positioning himself directly below, let it drop into his mouth, through his body, and onto the floor.

Lil pulled out a pencil, scribbled the Silverman details down on a serviette, stuffed it in her pocket and then chewed the end of the pencil excitedly. 'What do you think, Nedly?' she whispered. 'Murder? Maybe the caretaker was right; Silverman was pushed, maybe by an invisible hand. We've been waiting for weeks for

Gallows to put another spook into play. This could finally be it.'

'Sounds like nobody knows for sure,' Nedly said uncertainly.

'But it's worth looking into, right?'

He shrugged. 'OK. We better go and tell Abe.'

Lil chewed on a chunk of pencil woodpulp. 'Maybe.'

'He said if we heard anything we should let him know right away.' Nedly blew another olive into the air. It missed his open mouth and fell through his eyeball instead. He blinked, disconcerted.

'I don't see why we should do all the talking.' Lil slumped down in her seat. 'If he has anything, he's not letting on.' She twirled the pencil expertly for two turns and then dropped it on the floor.

'Maybe he doesn't have anything?'

'Then what's keeping him so busy?' She reached down for the pencil, patting the tiles blindly until she made contact. 'I know he's got to make ends meet but he can't be that tied up with bread-and-butter cases.' She made a grab for the pencil, stuck it back in her mouth and then took it out again quickly. It was a different pencil. 'It's just, the Gallows case, it's all we've got now and I thought we were going to try to track him down together . . .'

Nedly nodded.

Lil let her head fall back with a disappointed huff. 'What I mean is, for a while, it was like we were a proper investigative team, me, you and Abe and now it's just . . .'

'You and me.'

Lil winced. 'I didn't mean it like that.'

'I know. It's OK – I miss him too.'

'I know you do.' Her face brightened. 'Hey, maybe you should drop by later and see what he's up to – I mean, check he's OK.'

'Abe doesn't really like me going to his office without you.'

'I know, and I respect that. That's why it will be better if you arrive later when he has gone. Say, ten-thirty p.m.?'

'But what if he's still there?'

'Nobody works that late, and even if he is,

he won't know that you're there too.'

Nedly shifted uncomfortably in his seat. 'What if I give him the creeps? Anyway, Margaret will know.'

'Margaret wouldn't give you away; she loves you.'

'Do you think so?'

The look of almost tearful joy in his eyes made Lil bury hers in the melted cheese. 'Of course she does.'

'She always peels her lips back when she sees me, and her eyes sort of glare.'

'That's just how she smiles.'

Nedly pulled his neck in shyly. 'All right then. I'll go.'

'I don't know why you asked for olives if you were just going to throw them on the floor.' Velma had suddenly appeared, looking cross.

'But I . . . Sorry, I dropped them,' Lil mumbled, shooting a glance at Nedly.

'I would believe that if I hadn't seen you throw one up in the air first.'

'I didn't throw it in the air.'

'Then who did?'

Lil gritted her teeth. 'OK, it was me. Sorry.'

Nedly had been stationed at the window for twenty minutes before he saw the old brown Datsun pull up outside, its yellow headlights scouring the snow.

'Your mum's here!' he yelled to Lil. 'I'll meet you in the car!'

Lil ran to get her coat and scarf and Yoshi loaded her up with a box of that day's unwanted pastries and yesterday's muffins. Velma looked in the till, then took out the cash drawer, looked under it and sighed.

'Here.' She pushed a fiver into Lil's hand. 'We're a bit short tonight. It must be the snow, no one wants to come out in the evenings. Can we owe you?'

'The amount I've eaten tonight, I should probably be paying you,' Lil confessed. 'Things will pick up. I know they will.'

She paused at the door, looking out into the snowy street at her mother's profile in the car, and Nedly sitting behind her, looking contented. There was something wonderful and ordinary about the scene. Even though Naomi didn't know he was there.

'Did you forget something?' Velma called out.

'No, it's OK. Goodnight!'

Hench unlocked a door in the old town, using a dirty handkerchief to silence the bell. Under his arm he gripped a rolled-up towel. In his other hand was a torch. Sweat clung to the dark stubble on his bulky jaw.

As he entered the workshop he was met by an icy draught. Whispers floated on the night air, floorboards creaked and his torch flickered to a dim glow. He hurried past the rows of shelves crowded with dismembered plastic body parts, lines of china heads with unblinking eyes, and pots of dried-up glue.

He placed the towel on the heavy wooden workbench and carefully unrolled it. The small cloth poppet had turned grey and mouldy-looking.

Hench carried it to a glass-fronted display cabinet. Inside, the other poppets were lined up on the shelf, each made of the same cloth and yarn. One had black beads instead of crosses for its eyes.

He added the new poppet to the end of the line-up.

'There you go, Mr Dose,' he sniggered nervously, propping it up at the end of the shelf. 'Welcome home.'

He surveyed the line of poppets. 'Poisoner, swindler, mugger . . .' His eyes lingered on the overly wide stitched mouth and the black-beaded eyes of the first poppet in the row. 'Murderer.'

The poppet fell sideways and its bell tinkled softly. Hench's hand began to shake as he carefully righted it.

A door slammed somewhere behind him.

'Stay back,' he growled, and then he heard a noise from outside, the soft flumping sound of something taking a tumble in the snow. Hench left the cabinet door open and moved towards the window to have a look. He was almost there when the telephone rang out.

He picked up the receiver with sweaty palms. 'Yes, boss?'

Gallows' high voice came over the line. 'Mr Crank managed to convince Silverman to end it all?'

Hench gave a dutiful chuckle. 'He needed a bit of encouragement but Crank got right under his skin, so to speak. He can be very persuasive, am I right?' His gaze strayed to the deadpan face of the third poppet in the row and then fled down to the safety of the floor. 'I bribed the cops for the CCTV tape and dropped it off at the *Herald* offices, just like you said. This one will give them the heebies and no mistake.'

'Excellent. Now, who's next on my list? Ah yes, I suspect that our friend at the top here is going to sing. Maybe he didn't take my threat seriously?'

'Put the frighteners on him?' Hench said eagerly.

'Take him out of the game. He has exhausted his usefulness to me. Send Mr Bonce.'

Hench's bright blue eyes drifted back over to the cabinet, to a poppet with a disproportionately large head.

'Yes, boss.' He put the receiver down and reached across the poppets. As his hand moved over the first in the row he paused, fingertips trembling.

Hench resisted. 'Not you.' He avoided the glare of the poppet's black-bead eyes. 'Boss says you have to stay here until you do what you're told.'

Plucking Mr Bonce from the shelf before carefully closing the cabinet, he turned to the doorway and rattled the poppet three times.

'Here, boy,' he said.

Lil poked some apple peel through the bars of her hamster Waldo's cage and broke him off a bit of the muffin she was eating. The hamster took the offerings solemnly in his little pink paws and stowed them away in his nest, then he took a couple of turns on his wheel to work up an appetite.

'Lil!' her mother called from the kitchen. 'There's a cup of cocoa in here with your name on it.'

'Be right there!' Lil called back. On the way she swiped the pile of junk mail off the side table in the hall and sorted through it until she found the menu for the Black Pug Eatery. She extracted the evening edition of the *Klaxon* from between its pages and stuffed it into her back pocket.

Lil knew that you could get in a lot of trouble in Peligan City if you were found with a copy of the contraband news pamphlet, but the truth was, Naomi Potkin seemed oblivious to the *Klaxon* and the real news that its underground network of reporters revealed to its subscribers. She just kept her head down and squirrelled long hours away at the Public Records Department in City Hall. So many hours that Lil had got used to not having her around. So it had been strange when, a few weeks earlier,

Naomi had begun to spend more time at home, and ironic that by then Lil was so busy herself that it hadn't made much difference.

When Lil walked into the kitchen Naomi was sitting at the table, two mugs of steaming cocoa in front of her, hands steepled and head bowed in thought.

'Thanks, Mum!' Lil planted a quick kiss on her cheek, took the mug that said 'Lil' on it and started making for the door. 'Goodnight!'

Naomi looked up after her. 'I thought maybe we could sit and drink it together?'

Lil paused. 'I was going to take it up with me. I've got some study to do, for my correspondence course.' The former mayor had taken the controversial decision to close Peligan City's high schools the year after he closed the public libraries and the only education that Lil had received over the last two years was through the post, and it took all of her pot-washing money to pay for it.

'Oh, well, of course.' The disappointment in

38

her mother's voice was overruled by the sudden breezy smile that followed as she added, 'Goodnight then, little love.'

Naomi Potkin listened to her daughter's footsteps as they travelled up two flights of stairs to her attic bedroom. Then she raised her mug at the empty chair beside her, and said: 'Well, here's looking at you, kid,' and took a sip of cocoa. A two-tone horn blared through the darkness and the pans started humming on their hooks, the plates clinked against each other in the cupboards, and then the whole house shook as the train rattled past, its steel heart pounding against the tracks as it sped out of town like it was running for its life.

As the sound of the train faded away, Lil switched on her light, kicked off her shoes, drew the blind and then sat at her desk, flattening the *Klaxon* out in front of her.

It was too early for the Silverman suicide to appear. That was still breaking news. The centre pages carried a story about the continuation of the prison epidemic and the doctor locked in with the sickly inmates.

Sentenced to Death?
Editorial comment by Randall Collar

The prisoners in the Secure Wing for the Criminally Insane in Fellgate Prison are still in isolation under the instruction of prison doctor Alector Lankin and now it seems the mystery illness has claimed another victim.

With no access to the quarantined area it's impossible to report accurately on the situation at Fellgate, but one thing is certain – this epidemic shows no signs of going away and although the lockdown may prevent it spreading, this can be no comfort to those trapped inside. Governor Minos should be under increasing pressure to take action and yet the authorities seem to be happy to let it run its course as one by one the inmates succumb.

Perhaps it's time to think the unthinkable:

that Acting Mayor Gordian is reluctant to interfere because it makes financial sense to lessen the burden on the city's already overcrowded prison by allowing these inmates to die?

Lil cut out the article and stuck it to her wall with all the other clippings from the stories that Randall Collar had written, and then she carried on reading until her eyelids grew too heavy and the print began to swim. At 10.25 p.m. Lil glanced at her clock, rested her head on one arm and fell asleep there at her desk, under the beam of the Anglepoise lamp.

Chapter 4

The Toymaker

The ghostly glow of a reflected street lamp bounced off the windows of 154c Wilderness Lane, the address for Abe Mandrel's private investigations office. Nedly climbed up the old stairwell where the carpet had worn to dangerous threads in some places and one of the steps had been replaced with an ill-fitting old floorboard only slightly less rotten than the original stair would have been.

When he reached the third landing he faced

the frosted glass with the newly repainted lettering announcing 'Mandrel Investigations'. He wiggled his shoulders and then, grimacing, stuck his head through the door.

The street lamp outside shone through the slats of the blind that covered the window, striping the room with a cold pearly light. The newly acquired sagging leather settee where Abe sometimes slept was empty.

With a slurping sound Nedly's body followed his head through the door and he made straight for the desk, where he could see files with papers spilling out. He summoned all his energy into the Anglepoise lamp that hung over the desk, and with a hum it came on. He gave himself an encouraging thumbs up. Laid out beside the files was a street map covered in crosses, and pinned to one corner was the mugshot of Cornelius Gallows. A note was stuck to it, which read simply, 'WHERE IS HE?' Nedly was just about to try to flap up the cover of one of the files to peer inside when he heard a low rumbling growl.

Instinctively he ducked down behind the desk

and then slowly stood up again. A small sand-coloured mongrel stared up at him.

'Hey –' he began.

With the hair on her back all spiked up, Margaret looked like a miniature sharp-eared hyena. She flashed the whites of her eyes and her top lip began to curl, revealing tiny sharp teeth.

Nedly's own eyes widened in return. 'Hey, Margaret –' he tried again, trying to keep the tremble out of his voice.

Margaret emitted another low growl and pinned her ears flat to her head. Nedly held out a hand towards her and took a faltering step. Margaret stepped up the revs. Nedly put his foot back where it had come from.

Abe's voice came from the bathroom. 'What is it, girl?'

Nedly raised his finger to his lips. 'Shhhh!' he whispered, eyes darting to the door. 'Please, don't rat me out. I'm just here to see if Abe needs our help. I know you can't understand me, but I mean you no harm.' He backed away

a little more. Margaret's ears pricked up; she tilted her head to one side. 'That's a girl!' Nedly beamed and moved forward again. Margaret peeled her lips all the way back until her little pointed fangs were on full display. 'OK – I'll just stay here in the corner. You won't even know I'm here.'

As he shrank back towards the desk the bulb in the Anglepoise went out with a *ping*.

There was a flushing sound followed by the running of water and then Abe Mandrel walked out of the bathroom. His broad chin was covered in grizzled stubble and he had dark shadows under his eyes.

'Everything all right out here?' He rubbed Margaret's head. 'Something got you spooked?'

Margaret's black eyes slid over to where Nedly stood.

Abe pummelled his own arms as though he was trying to knock the cold out of them. He tried to switch on the desk lamp but the bulb was dead and gone. He turned on the overhead light instead and started rummaging through drawers, looking for a replacement bulb. A cold sweat was beading on his brow. Nedly pressed himself into the space by the window.

Outside, snow was swirling thickly from the ink-black sky. A lone figure in a corduroy cap hurried along the pavement, hustled by a gusting wind that flapped her tatty coat-tails and pulled at her apron strings. Reaching the corner she skidded on a patch of ice and fell over. Groping frantically in the snow for her glasses, she found them, then scrambled back onto her feet.

She splashed through the slush and then, turning head-on into the blizzard, crossed onto Wilderness Lane and rang the buzzer for number 154c.

Nedly had to spring out of the way as Abe prised open the blades of the blind to see who was there. He sighed and pressed the door release.

'Show them in, will you?' he said to Margaret, and opened the frosted-glass door to let her out.

Margaret cast a last cynical look at Nedly and then tippy-toed her way out of the office and down the stairs.

Abe took a moment to look at his reflection in the cracked glass of his framed but expired private detection certificate. He rubbed his chin wearily with his left hand, blinked his bloodshot eyes and then slapped himself awake with his rubbery right palm. He straightened his owl-patterned tie, smoothed down his hair and then he sat at his desk. He looked mournfully into the bottom of his mug and downed whatever remained there with a shudder.

The old woman followed Margaret back into the office. Thin but crimped grey hair radiated from her head like ripples of cold seawater. Her face had the colour and texture of a dried fig, with a determined mouth and large expressive eyes that blinked a lot behind thick plastic-framed glasses.

She held her corduroy cap in one trembling hand and stepped forward. 'I'm Yaroslava the toymaker,' she told Abe. Her other hand was outstretched in frayed fingerless gloves. It was red with cold and the joints were swollen. Abe shook it gently with his rubber one.

She was momentarily taken aback by the unexpected texture. 'What's that you've got there?' She blinked at him.

'It's a prosthetic,' Abe explained.

'Hmmm.' She peered at it. 'Can't do much with it like that. Do the fingers even bend?'

'The rubber hand is just for looks,' said Abe. Pulling it off and revealing the Swiss Army hand beneath, he unfolded some of the tools and displayed them in a fan shape. 'See, here I have a driving attachment, pen grip, letter opener, pliers, screwdriver . . .' He didn't mention the lock picker or the hot-dog holder.

The old woman nodded approvingly and took the seat opposite the desk, taking a firm hold of her own hands to stop them from shaking.

'It's cold out there,' she tried to explain. 'I could use something strong.' She raised her eyebrows at Abe hopefully.

'Strong coffee is the best I can do these days,

old-timer,' he replied. 'But it's good and hot . . .
at least it was.' He felt the jug. 'It's strong, at
any rate.'

'So,' he continued, 'you didn't come out here
at this late hour to talk about my hand.'

'I did not.' The toymaker rummaged in the
wide pocket of her apron and pulled out a
dog-eared card. It read: 'Absolom Mandrel,
Private Investigator. Civil – Domestic – Criminal
No case too small. Fully licensed, round-the-
clock service'. The address was beneath it.

Abe sighed. That card was years old.

'I got this from the landlord over at the Mingo,
it's a two-bit dive for end-of-the-roaders.'

'I've heard of it.'

'Indeed. You live there. In the basement.'

'I have a suite.' Abe tried to sound sure about
that.

The toymaker made a cheeky *hmpfh* noise.

No sooner had he passed her the coffee than
the woman knocked it back, greedily wiped her
mouth and held the mug out for another. Abe
tipped a second slug into it and then waited.

'When you're ready, Ms . . . Toymaker,' he said. 'Tell me what I can do for you.'

Margaret took up a position at the foot of the chair and stared intently at the toymaker, who blinked nervously.

'Don't mind Margaret,' Abe said, flipping open his notebook and clicking on his pen. He cleared his throat. 'So . . . you're a toymaker?'

'In a manner of speaking. For many years I have worked at the doll hospital out on Hen Road. Do you know it?'

'I've heard of it.'

'I have spent most of my life fixing broken limbs, sewing tiny clothes, pasting eyes back in and threading hair, but now people don't even have the money to repair their toys. The doll hospital was closed down several months ago. I couldn't afford the rent, you see?'

'Right,' said Abe quietly, unclicking the pen and resting it on the pad.

'So, it should be empty. But it's not. A man is there. He arrives at all times of the day and night.' She wagged a crooked finger at Abe.

'There is something funny going on. I don't know what he's up to but I don't like the look of him.'

Abe closed his eyes and massaged the bridge of his nose. 'What does he look like?'

'He is a thick-set man, with a potato-shaped head covered in curls of oily black hair. His jaw is wide and dusted with short black stubble, and several of his stubby fingers bear chunky gold rings. His suit is expensively cut but made of garish orange tweed with yellow threads, and he wears a ridiculous tiny hat that is much too small for his head.'

'You have an impressive eye for detail.'

'I do,' agreed the toymaker. 'But the most notable thing about him is his eyes. They are tiny and close together but they sparkle blue, like sapphires.'

Abe added 'blue eyes' to the mental list, which so far contained: average height, overweight, dark hair, money. 'So what did this man want?'

The toymaker shrugged dramatically. 'Who knows! Not me. They've changed the locks – suddenly I'm not allowed in there any more.'

'Could this man, the one you don't like the look of, could he be the new owner of the doll hospital?'

The toymaker snorted. 'Possibly. But isn't it more likely that he is up to no good – perhaps even stealing?'

Abe stifled a yawn in his sleeve.

'And that's not all,' the toymaker continued desperately, 'the place, it's changed. It's not welcoming to me. It's like it's . . .' She paused and flapped her hands in the air a couple of times, unable to find the words. The coffee pot gave a menacing gurgle, making everyone jump. Nedly pushed himself further into the corner.

Abe glanced round and loosened his collar. 'What kind of business do you think this new person is in?'

'Same business. Toys. I saw a whole boxful, newly arrived. Strange toys, not toys for children.'

Abe shifted uncomfortably in his chair. 'Look, I'm sorry you lost your job.'

'Whole life.'

'Well, all right, that too. But has any crime been committed?'

The toymaker shrugged. 'Don't ask me, I'm just a poor toymaker. You're the investigator: investigate.'

'I'll do it!' Nedly offered without thinking.

Margaret cocked her ears and stared at the apparently empty corner while the light bulb over the desk flickered. The toymaker's gaze shot around the room. Nedly clamped a hand over his mouth and then stuffed his hands into his pockets. He closed his eyes, willing the light to stay on and tried to sink further into the wall.

Abe closed his notebook and stole a glance at his watch. 'Is that the end of the story?' he asked hopefully. The toymaker nodded. 'OK, let me get this straight. The case you want me to investigate is someone, maybe even the owner of the premises, occupying the building, but not specifically taking or damaging anything that you can name, but nevertheless you think something is going on.'

The toymaker hesitated. She looked as though she wanted to add something, but it was something she was afraid to say out loud and so she agreed, 'That's the gist of it, detective.'

'OK, I'll tell you what, I'll look into it, and let you know if I find anything.'

'That's what the police said.'

'I'll bet.'

The old woman stood up and turned to go, but stopped mid-step. She let her head bow for a second and then with a stiff breath she pulled her coat round her and tightened her belt.

Abe got up out of his chair. 'Are you all right? Is there anything else? Something you aren't telling me?'

The toymaker looked down at her boots. 'I'm an old woman, detective. This cold goes right through my bones; sometimes I get the shivers – that's all.'

'Do you have somewhere to sleep tonight?'

'I'm going to head over to the shelter in St Bartholomew's. Don't worry about me.

Here.' She rummaged in her apron pocket

and pulled out a couple of coins and laid them on the table. 'For expenses.'

'Keep it. We'll settle up after. If there's anything in it,' he added.

'Very well.' She pocketed the coins again and pulled the cap back on over her hair. Abe held the door open for her. As she turned to go she said, 'Be careful, detective.'

Abe yawned discreetly into his collar. 'You can count on it.'

Chapter 5

The Doll Hospital

Lil put the kettle on to boil and dropped a couple of slices in the toaster. The breakfast things were all out on the table and the eggs were bobbing around in the pan like bald men in a Jacuzzi.

'Take a look at this article.' She pulled out a chair for Nedly to sit down on and spread out the morning edition of the *Klaxon* in front of him. 'Fresh off the press this morning.'

Investigation Terminated as Silverman
Death Recorded as Suicide

At 4 p.m. yesterday, Morpheus Silverman, chief financier at Peligan City Savings and Loans, died after falling forty-eight storeys from the roof of his former place of work. His body was discovered on the pavement below by bystanders moments later.

Police had been alerted to the incident shortly before when the building's alarm was set off. It was originally thought that an intruder had entered the building but no other person was found on the premises, so it is believed that Silverman himself may have activated the alarm. Although no suicide note has been located, Peligan City Police Department have closed the case after releasing a statement late last night maintaining that Silverman took his own life.

Silverman was known to have bankrolled some of the most controversial projects Peligan has ever seen, including the Golden Loop of super-casinos in the city centre. He *was also a major investor in the privatisation of Fellgate Prison and was rumoured to be behind a scheme to repurpose the old asylum on Bun Hill following a second fire there three months ago.*

Lil threw a couple of teabags in the pot. 'I think we should look Silverman up, while we're at the library. It sounds like he had his fingers in a lot of pies. If we cross-reference him with Gallows we might get a connection. Plus,' she added darkly, 'if our theory is correct and Gallows is up to his old tricks then he has another spook on his books. We should check the obituaries.'

Nedly nodded.

'So?' Lil swiped the *Klaxon* and returned it to her pocket, then sat down beside him with two rounds of freshly made toast, which she began cutting into soldiers. 'Fill me in. How did you get on at Abe's?'

'He was still there but I think I got away with it.' Nedly shifted uncomfortably.

'So, what did you get?'

'Maybe something, maybe nothing. This lady came in; she wanted Abe to go and check out this old doll hospital, out on Hen Road. She thought something was going on there.'

'What did you think?'

Nedly shrugged. 'I'm not sure Abe is going to follow it up but someone should – she seemed – *yurghk!*' His eyes jumped out of their sockets as Naomi whisked into the kitchen and pushed his chair back under the table, half embedding him amongst the breakfast things. Lil watched him disappear as he wilted to the floor.

'What did I think about what?' Naomi seemed completely unfazed by her proximity to Nedly; she showed no signs of the creeps most people felt, or the shiver-inducing icy chill. She stood, her hands still on the back of the chair, looking down at Lil with a worried frown.

Lil shuffled through possible clever comebacks and settled on a weak 'I thought you'd gone to work already?'.

'I'm leaving now. So who were you talking to?'

'Myself.'

Naomi gave her a considered look. 'Are you OK?'

'Fine. I was –' What *was* she doing? 'I was just running some lines from this film we saw yesterday at the picture house.'

'We? You've made a friend who likes the same films you do?' Naomi looked amazed. Lil rolled her eyes; it wasn't that unlikely. 'That's great!' She gave Lil's chin a soft pinch and tilted her head up so she could look her in the eye. 'So, does this new friend have a name?'

'Nedly.'

'Very unusual. What's he like?'

'He's great.' Lil glanced down to where Nedly was sitting under the table, his arms wrapped round his knees, looking traumatised. 'He's . . . different.'

'Well.' Naomi tucked Lil's hair behind her ears and gave her a kiss on the forehead. 'I'm really glad. You should invite him round some time. We could get a pizza in and all watch a film together.'

Lil smiled: they had done that a couple of times already. 'Sure.'

'Well, OK then. Have to fly now.'

Lil waited until she heard the squeal of the ancient fan belt from her mum's car and then ducked down to check on Nedly. 'It's OK. She's gone.'

He crawled out and brushed the non-existent crumbs off his jeans. He was smiling widely now.

Lil grinned back without knowing why. 'What's funny?'

'Nothing, it's just, your mum!'

'I know.' Lil snorted. 'She's so weird.'

Nedly shook his head, still beaming. 'No, I mean, she knows my name now; she knows I exist.'

Hen Road was just round the corner from the Picture House on Spooner Row. It was a quiet area of small-scale warehouses and lock-ups, most of which were closed down and out of business, so the snowfall was untrodden until

Lil left her footprints there as she and Nedly approached their destination.

Its frontage was shop-like with a small door and a large window, across which the words 'Peligan City Doll Hospital' had once been neatly painted, although now the lettering was chipped and turned dull with age. Lil cupped her eyes to block out the glare of the snow and suckered her hands onto the glass.

Inside the room were shelves, cabinets and chests, all full of the kind of toys that gave her the creeps: clockwork monkeys, jack-in-the-boxes and china dolls, but after Wool, the toy Gallows had used to bind his first ghost, Mr Glimmer, all toys had taken on a sinister shade for Lil.

At the back of the room was a workbench with a magnifying lamp bent over it and sitting there was a man in a loud checked suit and a pork-pie hat. He was holding a limp figure in one of his stubby hands and in the other he had a needle and thread.

'That must be the new owner,' Nedly whispered.

Lil tried the door handle. It was locked. She

rattled it a few times. The new owner looked up and frowned. Lil put a harmless grin on her face as she waved at him and then knocked briskly on the window.

The man got to his feet, hefted his way over and opened the door, just enough to wedge his whole body in the gap. Nedly backed away out of range.

'Can I help you?' The toymaker had been right about his eyes, they were small and close, but a startling blue.

'Hey, mister,' Lil said brightly. 'Can I have my doll back? I brought it in for fixing a while ago.'

The man cocked his head to one side. 'Aren't you a bit old for toys?'

'It was quite a long while ago.'

He opened the door a little more. 'Why don't I get it for you? What does it look like?'

'If I could just get inside I'll find it.' Lil tried to sidestep him.

He stuck out his arm to block her path. 'No can do.' He smiled again. He was wearing enough cologne to make Lil's eyes water.

She tried a more direct approach. 'The old woman who used to run this place, I bumped into her the other day – that's what reminded me about my doll,' she added.

'That old bird! She's always hanging around here, sticking her beak where it doesn't belong, am I right?' It wasn't really a question but he punctuated it with a companionable jab to Lil's arm.

'Look, don't get me wrong, I feel sorry for her. The place obviously meant a lot, but this is my business now and I got a lot to do before I can reopen. Look at what a mess it is!'

Lil took the opportunity to peer over his arm. It was a mess.

'So –' his voice dropped to a conspiratorial level – 'she's been talking to you, has she?'

'No,' Lil replied honestly.

'Glad to hear it. The last thing any new businessman needs is someone putting out a bad word against him in the local community, am I right?' He gave Lil another quick jab and the blue eyes twinkled again. 'Now, you'll have to excuse me – I've got a lot to do. But come back in a couple of weeks, by then I'll have the place straightened out and we can reunite you with your precious doll, no problem! What's the point of all these toys with no kids to play with them, am I right?'

Lil ducked out of the reach of his hand and hit the pavement at a jog, calling over her shoulder: 'Thanks anyway!'

'My pleasure!' he called after her. 'And if you see that old toymaker, you tell her I said hello.' He froze there in the doorway for a few moments, hand raised in a wave.

Lil waited until they got to the corner before muttering to Nedly, 'What a knucklehead! I think maybe I'll come back when he's gone. Have a proper poke around.'

As they crossed the road and set off for the library, neither one saw the new owner's expression change as he lowered his hand. The sparkling eyes narrowed and the smile slipped from his face as easily as a greasy egg off a dirty plate.

Chapter 6

The Locked Door

Peligan City Library had been closed for more than a decade. Beneath the crumbling stone figures of the old gods of wisdom and knowledge that watched over it, the building was boarded up, its bricks darkened by algae, graffiti and exhaust fumes.

Inside was another story. Only a handful of people knew the access code, or the way in through the loose window in the courtyard, and they worked hard to keep its secrets until the day came that they could open its doors to the public once again. For as long as there is a librarian within its walls there will be a library and Logan MacKay had enough grit to outlast crooked mayors such as Tantalus Dean, who had shut this particular branch, and even those like Gordian who let it stay shut. And she wasn't alone.

Lil Potkin had been a frequent visitor since she was a tot, drawn to the great newspaper archive that it held, amongst other things. Lately she had started working some volunteer hours to help out, sorting and returning the newspapers that other people had been reading into their rightful places in the basement stacks. Apart from her own research, the only person Lil had ever seen using the library was Logan; nevertheless there were always plenty of papers to be refiled.

In the large circular reading room Nedly sat at one end of a polished wood table, rereading his way through an old edition of *More Adventure Comics!* They had found a whole box of them in the basement of the library. The green-glass lamp on the table flickered and dimmed softly each time a page wafted over.

Thwump! Lil dropped a muddled stack of *Herald*s down on the other end of the table with a thud, sending a ripple of echoes around the room. She laid them out in a row as though she was about to play a giant hand of Solitaire. The newspapers were only a few months old and the front pages mostly ran stories on the new legislation of the acting mayor, Police Commissioner Gordian, for the clean-up of the city.

Lil leafed through them, pausing as she came across a paper with the headline: '**Homelessness on the Decline in Peligan City!**'

'Really?' She frowned and scanned through the article. 'I thought it was getting worse. If you ask me, they're just cleaning up the city centre by moving all the problems to the outskirts. Nedly, we should have checked Delilah's doorway again! We'll go on the way home.'

She glanced over at where Nedly was sitting.

He was no longer absorbed in the comic, but glaring at one of her old chewed pencils and pointing his finger commandingly at it. Lil realised she had been talking to herself, maybe for a long while.

'Nedly?'

He looked up at her. 'Sorry. What?'

'What are you doing?'

'Just practising some moves.'

Lil watched the pencil roll haltingly across the desk. 'Does it help if you hold your hand out like that?'

Nedly shrugged. 'I think it focuses my energy.'

'Really?'

'I don't know,' he admitted. 'But it looks good, doesn't it?' The pencil rolled slowly off the edge of the desk and fell onto the floor.

Lil retrieved it. 'Where did you get the idea from, about focusing your energy like that?'

'It's just something that people do.'

'What people?'

'Just people.' Nedly went back to his comic book.

'Haven't you read that one a hundred times already?'

'Number fifty-three – it's the best one,' he explained. 'There's this guy, Tom Conaghan, and in the last issue he was killed by this hoodlum who had just got out of prison –'

Lil gasped suddenly. 'The prison! Of course!' And abandoned Nedly for the other side of the room. She rifled through one of the index boxes, pulled out a card, then ran back to the table and flicked through the corresponding papers to confirm her theory. 'That's the link! All these papers have a story on the Needle!'

She pushed them into a neatish stack. 'Which means that someone here at the library has been checking out the archive on Fellgate Prison. And there was that article in the *Klaxon* about the epidemic just last night . . .'

Nedly pursed his lips. He knew what was coming.

'So, who do you think has been checking them out?' Lil let her gaze drift knowingly towards the door of the librarian's office.

Nedly sighed. 'Not this again.'

'Just a tiny glimpse.'

'I already did that the first time you asked me, and the time after that, and the time after that, and I told you it's just an office.'

'I know it's an office but the big question is whose?' Lil tapped her chewed pencil against the side of her nose. 'It's the *Klaxon* HQ; I know it is. It's got to be in there. Are you sure you didn't see any files lying around?'

'Nothing.' He shrugged. 'There was a filing cabinet but it was locked, with a combination – like a safe.'

Lil sighed enviously. 'Sounds like top-secret stuff. Just like I suspected. Something's going on in there. Something they don't want anyone to know about.' Her eyes took on a dangerous gleam.

Nedly gave up on his comic. 'Why don't you just knock on the door and see if they'll let you in – now that you're on the staff, I mean?'

That smarted. 'You know why: no one ever answers. Except Logan that once.'

'So maybe, for now at least, the office is out of bounds.'

Lil stared at him.

'You know,' Nedly continued uncomfortably, 'snooping around and spying on crooks, that's OK, but spying on your friends . . .'

His words struck Lil like a slammed door. 'You don't want to help me?'

He sighed. 'No, I'll always help if you ask me to; I just wish that sometimes you wouldn't ask.'

Lil toyed with a grim smile she'd been working on, the one she would do if she got betrayed by a fellow journalist, but it wasn't the right moment so she let it fall. 'All right. That's fair I suppose. It's just that I can't help being curious, and sometimes I wish I could do the stuff you can do.'

Nedly looked at her gravely. 'No you don't.'

'No.' She chewed on her lip. 'I didn't mean that. Sorry.'

He gave her a lopsided smile. 'Anyway, if your theory is right, why would *Klaxon* reporters be using the *Herald* for information? You said it doesn't have any real news in it.'

Lil raised a finger in an *Ahhh!* 'I've revised my opinion on that. You see, the thing about the *Herald* is that the news is in there; it's just that it's buried, or spun so hard that it's difficult to see the real story. It's not what they're saying, it's what they're *not* saying that's important, and why they're not saying it. You have to read between the lines.'

Nedly stared at Lil.

'What?'

'You really sound like you know what you're talking about.'

'Do I? I mean, I do.' She drew in enough puff to make herself stand a bit taller. 'I may not be allowed in that office but I am a reporter myself now and I've been doing that correspondence course in journalism, looking at context and all that stuff.' She brushed away Nedly's admiring gaze with a bad attempt at an embarrassed shrug and heaved the stack of newspapers into her arms.

Nedly looked shyly down at the table. 'You know, I've been wondering too, about the future and everything.' Lil hoisted the bundle onto her hip and started staggering towards the lift. 'I know things will never be normal for me . . . because of my . . . condition.'

Lil carried on walking, even though the papers had suddenly become twice as heavy as they were a moment ago. Even though there was a tight feeling in her chest like someone was standing on it. She swallowed it all down and then said:

'Who wants "normal" anyway?' Her voice sounded thicker than she'd hoped for. She cleared her throat. 'Don't let that stop you. You deserve to have a shot, same as everyone else.'

Nedly overtook her at a jog and then wheeled round to catch her eye, strolling backwards. 'There's a little something I've been working on. Something maybe only I can do.'

As they stepped into the service lift a siren passed in the distance, breaking the silence of the library. They both listened until the sound had faded.

'So, are you going to tell me what it is?'

'I haven't got it all figured out yet, but as soon as I do you'll be the first to know.'

Lil knew she would be. 'Whatever it is, you'll be great at it.' She forced her lips into a grin. 'OK, now,' she said, nodding at the grille that had to be drawn across before the lift would work. 'Give it a go.'

Nedly took a deep breath and closed his eyes. Breathing out slowly he opened them again.

Swallowing back an impatient sigh Lil transferred the weight of the papers to her other arm.

Nedly glared at the grille, and the metal began to hum – Lil could feel the vibration in the soles of her feet – then it rattled violently. She flicked a look across at Nedly. His eyeballs were almost out of the sockets as the grille began to move at no more than an ant's pace, unfolding as it stretched.

Lil's arms were aching. 'Is that as fast as it will go?'

Cautiously Nedly raised his hand and pointed at it. The grille continued to creep along. The tip of his finger started glowing slightly, as though there was a strong light beneath the skin. The grille suddenly shot the last foot and slammed shut with a bone-shattering clang.

'Sorry,' Nedly winced. 'I lost control of it a bit at the end there. But I think this hand thing really does work.' He blew on the end of his finger and grinned.

Lil backed towards the control panel and pushed the 'down' button with her elbow. 'Either way, it was definitely better than last time.'

As they began their descent the trill of a ringing phone cut through the reading room. Lil's head whipped up, and she stared at the door to the librarian's office, holding her breath. The ringing stopped. They were only head and shoulders above floor level when the office door was suddenly flung open and they saw a knot of legs and feet hurry past, their footsteps pounding the carpet tiles.

'Whaaaat!!!' Lil watched them helplessly as she sank out of sight. She let the bundle of papers fall and then turned on Nedly. 'You said it was empty!'

'I said the last time I looked it was empty.'

'Then where have all those people come from? It's the *Klaxon* reporters, I know it is!' Lil slip-slid across the scattered *Herald*s and hammered on the 'stop' button. 'Quick! They're getting away!' The lift was barely stationary before she started pumping the 'up' button furiously and the machinery groaned in protest, the cogs reversed direction and they began their ascent.

Lil held on to the metal grille like a prisoner clings to the bars of their cell, willing the lift to pick up speed as they clanked slowly between floors. 'Nedly, quick follow them!'

'I will!' he cried. 'Just get the lift to the next floor.'

Lil gritted her teeth. 'You don't need to wait for the lift; you can just melt through the shaft, or something.'

Nedly gave her an incredulous look. 'It's a hole. I can't melt through a hole; there's nothing there to melt through.'

'Can't you just do that relocation thing?'

'That's not how it works. I can only do that to where you are and you're here.'

Lil gritted her teeth again. When the lift reached the reading room Nedly cast her a last disapproving look as he climbed up through the grille, then set off in pursuit.

'Don't let them get away,' she yelled.

When the lift finally reached the ground level she yanked the grille aside, but by then everyone was gone.

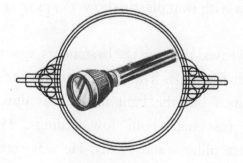

Chapter 7

Multi-Storey Murder

It didn't take Lil long to work out where they had gone to; she just followed the sound of sirens to where the snow was tinted ultraviolet with flashing blue lights. The multi-storey car park, a crate of grey concrete squatting against the plum-coloured sky was only three blocks away.

On the pavement beyond the cordon a murmuring crowd had gathered, but the police weren't letting anyone through. They stood sentry all down the line, dressed in hi-vis jackets with thin plastic shower caps over their hats.

Lil weaved through the bystanders, casing the cordon for gaps. The mouth of the car park was open but the light inside was dim. She could just make out low ceilings, ramps, concrete pillars, and Nedly. He was standing right at the entrance, waving to get her attention and then pointing towards the back of the crowd. Lil tried to subtly nod to him to go in to the car park and have a look at the crime scene but he either couldn't understand her, or he didn't want to.

'Hey!' he called out as he passed through the cordon, drawing shivers from two of the police officers who shrank away from each other, their eyes meeting in horror. The tightly packed crowd seemed to unzip before Nedly as he moved through it, towards Lil.

'Look!' He grinned excitedly. 'There's Abe!'

Leaning against a plaster pillar in an ornate but crumbling doorway was Abe Mandrel, watching the scene from under his battered trilby. Margaret sat by his feet, sheltering under his shabby old mac.

Abe looked up to meet Lil's gaze. He offered her a brief nod and his once-steely jaw stretched a fraction in a whisper of a smile.

'Aren't you supposed to be at the library?'

'I knocked off early.'

Abe pulled his collar up and buried his chin in it. He took a furtive glance around and then trying not to move his mouth he mumbled, 'Nedly,' and nodded at the strip of empty space beside Lil.

Nedly was actually crouching on the floor on her other side. 'Hey, Margaret!' He beamed at the little dog. Margaret sort of grinned back but it was a smile that showed all her teeth and set her back hair on end.

Lil tried to mirror Abe's casual pose against the pillar. 'So, what's happening?'

Abe gave the tableau before him a suspicious frown. 'No one knows. Something they were trying to hush up, but word got out. Then the cops arrived to keep everyone calm and caused a scene.'

'Maybe Nedly could go in and get a closer look?' Lil suggested.

Nedly backed away a little.

Abe shook his head grimly. 'There are some things you can't unsee. That guy over there.' He pointed his rubber hand at a squad car behind the police lines. 'He was the first on the scene.' The officer in question was sitting in the passenger seat, slumped over his knees, white-faced and with his head in his hands.

Without looking at Lil, Abe added, 'So, did you find anything interesting at the doll hospital?'

Lil shrugged. 'Not really,' and bobbed down to stroke Margaret. Then, realising her mistake, said, 'What doll hospital?'

Abe snorted. A black van from Peligan City morgue turned up and he watched it from under his hat for a moment and then added, 'If you want to know something just come out and ask me.'

Nedly turned an embarrassed shade of pewter and scowled at Lil.

A troop of scene-of-crime officers, dressed in white plastic jumpsuits with tight hoods and wellingtons, disappeared into the mouth of the car park like they were being drawn in by the beam of a UFO. From somewhere in the crowd a flashbulb blew and the cops scurried in to confiscate the camera.

A tall, suited man, with neat curls of silver hair and a duffle coat drifted over and stole Lil's spot leaning against the pillar beside Abe. Both men kept their eyes on the scene.

'Detective Mandrel,' the man murmured. 'You still working this town?'

Abe dropped his chin further into his collar. 'She's a tough client but I guess we're stuck with each other.'

Lil tried to lean nonchalantly on the spare pillar on the other side of the doorway but it was too far away to hear their hushed voices, so she ambled back towards them and settled for a free-standing casual spectator pose, with her back to the two men.

Abe took off his trilby and knocked the snow out of the dent. 'Lil,' he said, 'this is Dr Leon Monbatsu. He's the city pathologist.'

Lil glanced over her shoulder, gave a nod of acknowledgement and whispered, 'Lil Potkin.' Then added with a skip to her heartbeat, 'Reporter.'

Monbatsu made to walk away but Abe quickly added, 'She's OK; she's with me.' And he settled back down.

'Potkin.' Monbatsu murmured it like a question.

Abe cleared his throat. 'So, anything unusual about this one?'

Monbatsu examined the top toggle of his duffle. 'Oh, it's unusual all right, but these days they usually are.'

Bystanders jostled to get a look-in as a tow truck appeared in the mouth of the car park dragging a pearl-grey Bentley behind it. Behind the smashed windshield, Lil could just make out a blurred shape at the steering wheel as they drove away past the police lines.

'They're going to have to cut him out of there,' Monbatsu told them.

A wave of murmurs broke through the crowd, leaving a crushing silence in its wake as two of the white-suited figures steered a trolley down the ramp at the mouth of the car park. It was laden with a series of lumps strapped down under an orange plastic sheet.

'That's for me,' Monbatsu said grimly. Without a backwards glance he stepped away from the pillar. 'Good to see you again, detective. You should stop by for a drink sometime.' He reached in his pocket for his official pass. 'Perhaps 9 a.m. sharp tomorrow morning, if it suits you.'

As he drew level with Lil he whispered, 'The only newspaper in this town is the *Herald*, and the *Herald* haven't sent a reporter out to investigate a story since the day it was born. And if you don't write for the *Herald*' – he sharp-eyed her – 'then someone might ask, who do you write for?'

Lil's ears were glowing like beacons. She wanted to flatten her hair over them but she knew that would make her look even more suspect. She'd slipped up and she knew it, blown her cover just to look like the big 'I am'. The *Klaxon* had been a fiercely guarded secret for years; no one knew who the reporters were who wrote for it.

As she floundered, the air was filled with the deafening rattle of a freight train passing on the overhead lines, taking goods from the docks across to the mail line. Monbatsu was still waiting for an answer. She glanced sideways and up at him expecting to see something accusing in his eyes, but instead she saw a warning.

'No one,' she admitted finally. 'I was just joking around.'

'You're too young to be a reporter anyway,' Abe added.

Monbatsu nodded, satisfied, and said more loudly, 'I think we can safely assume there are no reporters here today.'

When he was out of earshot Lil shook her head and whispered to Nedly.

'There *are Klaxon* reporters here. There must be. We heard them get the call, saw the legs leave the office.' She gave him a quick glare. 'If only you'd jumped out of the shaft sooner, you could have I.D.d them.'

'I told you already, I can't . . .'

'Forget it,' Lil snapped, and then more softly she added, 'It's just that might have been our best shot, maybe our only chance. We were so close . . .' She let her gaze thread through the crowd, looking for likely undercover reporters. *Would they be in disguise?*

Her eye was met by a short man in a green waterproof poncho with an elasticated hood. He was wearing orange tinted aviator spectacles and had a small, neat goatee beard. He stood out like a sore thumb, but maybe it was a double bluff, maybe he was hiding in plain sight?

Lil's field of vision was suddenly infiltrated by a small familiar figure making their way towards them, with a huge lilac scarf wound round their neck.

'Mum?' Naomi's hair was fuzzed and strung

with droplets of melted snow and her glasses were steamed up white; it was a miracle she could see at all. 'What are you doing here?'

Naomi took off her glasses and wiped the lenses with the end of her scarf. 'I was just cutting through on my way to somewhere else; how about you?

Lil tried to shrug casually. 'The same. Only the police have closed the road so . . .'

Abe sidled up to them and tipped his hat. He was standing up very straight all of a sudden and his belly looked like it had been sucked up into his chest.

'Hello, Abe.' Naomi twinkled her eyes at him.

Abe, who had run out of puff almost instantly, managed to wheeze, 'Good to see you, Naomi.' He nodded at the car park. 'What do you make of all this?'

The mortuary van doors were shut and the driver pulled away. Under her breath Naomi told them: 'It's Governor Minos. He's been murdered.'

'Minos? The guy who runs the prison?' Lil gave her mum a disbelieving frown. Naomi shook it off. 'I heard a couple of people talking as I walked by.'

'High-profile,' said Abe. 'That explains all the cops.'

Naomi continued, 'His driver was dead on arrival too, at the wheel of his car. They were found on the top floor. I heard someone say that the murder was likely to have taken place last night.'

Lil murmured to Nedly, 'She heard all that just walking through the crowd? We've been standing in the wrong place.'

Abe forced a deep breath out through his nose. 'Nasty business.' He tapped the snow out of his hat again and took the opportunity to smooth down his hair.

'Lil?' Her mother touched her lightly on the arm. 'I was thinking, tonight maybe we could get a takeaway, see if there's anything good on the TV?'

Lil glanced across at her. She wondered if her mum would really be there when she got back. Maybe she would.

'Yeah,' she said. 'That would be nice.' Her eye was caught again by a movement in the crowd. The man in the green poncho was looking their way, his hand raised in what looked like a wave, but then he was swallowed up in the rush as the police started clearing the streets, pushing the cordon back and sounding short bursts of their sirens.

Abe contemplated the multi-storey as the bystanders in front of it dispersed. 'What I'd like to know is what was Minos doing here in the first place?'

Naomi rewrapped her scarf, rubbed the snow out of Lil's hair and gave her a kiss on the cheek, then she started off towards the crowd, pausing just before she vanished to look over her shoulder and say, 'Maybe he was meeting someone.'

Abe watched her go.

Nedly shuddered. 'What kind of person do you meet in a deserted car park in the dead of night?

Lil let her gaze drift upwards until she was

squinting into the falling snow. 'Someone you don't want anyone else to know about.'

In the prison doctor's office, deep in the Secure Wing for the Criminally Insane in the belly of the Needle, Hench pulled a strip of burnt vinyl wallpaper away and let it drop to the floor.

'This place smells like death. I don't know how you can stand it.' He cursed as he saw the black sooty dust on his hand and tried to wipe it off on the back of the door, which was almost as dusty. His fingertips rippled over the series of long grooves in the wood, eight shallow nail marks where Dr Hans Carvel had, not so long ago, tried unsuccessfully to escape Mr Glimmer's inferno. Hench shuddered and buried his dirty hand in his pocket.

'Did it ever occur to you to redecorate?'

Gallows looked at the melted walls with their bubbling wallpaper as though he were seeing them for the first time and shrugged. 'There's something cosily familiar about this room. I will be sorry to leave it but Dr Lankin's time is almost at an end too. Once the harvest is complete the brave doctor must mysteriously disappear.'

He stopped to think this over. 'Or maybe his body will be found, burnt beyond recognition, just to tie up the loose ends. But of course I have used that method already for faking my own death. It's so tempting to stick to the old tried-and-tested routines, knowing that people will fall for it, just as they always do. Ramon taught me that.' He pricked up his ears to tune in to the quivering sobs that came from the last cell in the row where Ramon LeTeef, his treacherous old partner in crime, was incarcerated.

Gallows sighed. 'But if all my great acts are to be recorded in history, which they surely will be, I should at least try to think of something more ingenious.' He rested his chin in one cupped hand and let the elbow of his already filthy lab coat pick up more soot from the table.

'Of course it really won't matter. As soon as City Hall is mine, I, alone, will decide what is investigated and what isn't.'

Hench cleared his throat and Gallows looked up sharply as though he had forgotten the other man was there. 'What is it you want, Hench?'

'I thought you should know: the death of Minos has attracted a lot of attention.'

Gallows' cold eyes lit up. 'Excellent. It was a brazen move on my part but it was time, time the people of Peligan City realised what they are up against. We handed it to them in black and white on those CCTV tapes of Silverman's demise and those fools down at the *Herald* just sat on it! What's wrong with the press in this city? How many more kingpins have to die before someone considers it newsworthy?' He totted up the figures in his head and then sighed irritably. 'It's almost as though someone is attempting to cover my tracks.' He stroked his hairless chin with a fingernail that had grown long and dirty. 'I had to place several anonymous tip-offs myself. They may have covered up Silverman and the others but surely they can't fail to raise the alarm now that Mr Bonce has snuffed out Governor Minos in his own inimitable style.' He rapped his knuckles on the desk thoughtfully. 'Yes, it's high time indeed to initiate the end game.'

Hench looked bewildered and Gallows sighed. 'Peligan City is still suffering under the illusion that things are under control. Let's make sure everyone knows that they aren't.

'Activate the Weasel! Once the lily-livered general public realise are they are at the mercy of my bogeymen, those clowns at City Hall will be desperate to find someone to bring order to this chaos. That is when I shall appear. Terror is the mechanism by which I will bring Peligan to its knees!'

Gallows sank awkwardly to his own bony knees on the stone floor and triumphantly pounded the air above him with loosely formed fists. He stayed there for a moment basking painfully in his future glory and then pulled himself up by the outside seam of Hench's trousers.

Once he was on his feet Gallows clicked his fingers. 'Get me the hit list.'

Hench placed a grubby page covered in scrawl

into Gallows' hand. As his gaze travelled through the list he murmured a few names to himself and then his eyelid twitched. 'Ping.' He pushed the word out through his teeth. 'She's next.'

Hench gulped and dabbed at his face with his handkerchief. 'Who shall I send? Mr Dose?'

Gallows pondered this. 'Or has Mr Grip been punished enough?'

'Not Grip.' Hench shook his head like he was trying to get free of something.

'He frightens you.' Gallows' thin lips stretched gleefully.

'You don't have to be around him all the time; you don't feel it like I do.'

Gallows sighed. 'Our relationship is different. You keep their poppets but I gave them life, in a manner of speaking. I am their father. You are more like a blithering cousin from out of town who they tolerate because I have told them to.'

'Grip is a troublemaker. He's always watching, always waiting.' Hench's voice was trembling now.

'Perhaps.' Gallows' eyes shone. 'But there's

nothing quite like a murderer to give people the heebie-jeebies. No doubt he loathes you, Hench, but I will always have his gratitude. Before he met me he was trapped in an old man's body, locked away. And now he's free. Well, in a manner of speaking.'

Hench pushed a fat finger round the collar of his shirt, where his neck bulged over. 'I don't trust him.'

Gallows smirked. 'How clever of you. Of course, you would be best advised not to trust any of them.' He sighed impatiently. 'If Grip is getting too big for his boots, keep him on the shelf for a couple more days; show him who's in charge.'

Hench's sapphire-blue eyes sparkled. 'Yes, boss,' he said, with an oily grin.

Chapter 8

The Dog Who Wouldn't Play Ball

At eight thirty the next morning Abe answered the persistent knocking at his office door to find Lil standing on the other side of it.

'How did you get up here?'

'The catch on the front door is busted, so I just walked in.' She wrinkled her nose at him. 'I thought you'd be ready by now. What's that on your face? Is it cream?'

'It's shaving foam, obviously.' He eyed her suspiciously. 'Ready for what?'

'Our appointment at the morgue is for 9 a.m., isn't it?

'My appointment.' He spread his bulk across the doorway, blocking Lil from entering, but inadvertently drawing attention to the hot-water bottle that he had fastened to his belly with his palm-tree-print tie. 'You better find something else to do; a building full of stiffs is no place for a kid.' He caught Lil staring at the hot-water bottle and folded his arms to cover it.

'If Gallows is behind it, then it's my case too,' said Lil, slipping in past the gap that he'd left. Nedly followed, making Abe shudder.

'What if it's a lead to a different case?'

'There's only one way to find out.' Lil helped herself to a Danish from a plate on the sideboard. 'Rikes!' she spluttered through a mouthful of greasy crumbs. 'How old is this?' She spat the elderly pastry into the bin and dusted the rest of it off her palms. 'You probably heard all about Silverman?' Abe nodded. 'So this is the second mysterious death in Peligan in as many days and Monbatsu said there was something weird going on. I want to find out what. Just as much as you do,' she added, giving him the Squint.

Abe sighed. 'Fine.' He took out a pocket comb and tried to decide if his hair had a parting.

'Why are you getting all dolled up anyway?'

Abe blushed down to his roots. 'I'm not getting dolled up; I'm just making myself presentable.'

'For the morgue?'

'I've got plans later.'

'What plans?' Lil gave him the Squint again.

Abe folded under it. 'Nothing really, just Naomi and I . . . you know, your mother –'

'I know who Naomi is.'

'Right. Well, me, and Naomi, we'll probably grab a coffee or something. Over at the Nite Jar. It's no big deal. I'm not making big deal of it. Just two friends, catching up on old times. Nothing more to it than that.'

'Like a date?'

'No, not a date.' Abe gave a desperate-sounding laugh and loosened his collar, and then his face became serious. 'Why, did she tell you it was a date?'

'She didn't tell me anything about it.'

'No, well, like I said. It's no big deal.' Abe tried an offhand shrug to cover the glow that was creeping over his cheeks. 'We'll just be chewing the fat. About you, probably – she's worried. She's heard you talking to Nedly and now she thinks you have an invisible friend.'

Lil and Nedly looked at each other.

'I do have an invisible friend.'

Abe unhooked his mac from the coat stand and forced the arm with the prosthetic hand down a sleeve that was still pulled inside out from the last time he'd taken it off. 'She means one that isn't real – an imaginary person.'

'But I've already told her that Nedly is real. I mean, I've told her that I've got a friend, and that his name is Nedly.'

'Does she know he's invisible?'

Lil sighed. 'Not yet.' She smiled sympathetically at Nedly and shivered. The only warm things in the office were the coffee maker on the side, oozing the smell of burning plastic, and a little electric fire ticking away in the corner by Margaret's bed, but neither one did much to take the chill out of the air.

Lil turned to the coffee machine. 'Can I have a cup of this to warm me up?'

Abe shrugged. 'Knock yourself out.'

She peered into the jug of steaming java. 'This looks like it's been brewing since you bought that Danish. There's sort of a skin on it, and it's thick, like oil,' she said. 'Is that how it's supposed to look?'

Abe pushed his lips out into a duckbill pout. 'It's my coffee and that's how I like it.' To prove his point he poured himself a shot and slung it back. He tried to gulp but his throat didn't seem to want to let it in.

Abe thumped himself on the chest a couple of times to knock the stuff down. It was so strong it made him sweat. He wiped his face on the back of his hand and realised he was still covered in shaving foam. Frowning, he left the room to use the sink in the small bathroom.

'You should really get the radiator fixed,' Lil yelled over the groaning of pipes as he ran the taps.

'Just as soon as I get a piece of serious work from a paying client I will,' he yelled back. 'Anyway, I don't feel the cold.' Lil heard the hot-water bottle flopping to the floor.

Nedly was smiling excitedly at Margaret. 'Lil, check it out – Margaret is sort of smiling at me. What do you say, girl? Is that a smile for your old pal Nedly?'

Lil looked at Margaret's wide, staring eyes and the clump of hair that stood up on her haunches. Her black lips curled back, revealing neat white teeth.

'Sure,' said Lil.

'I think I'm growing on her,' said Nedly, making out like he was ruffling her fur but from a couple of metres away. 'She was just nervous, that's all.' He took a step towards her.

Margaret growled.

'Come on, Margaret,' Lil whispered under her breath. 'Give him a break.'

'I give her the creeps, I know. It's OK.' He looked like he was trying to shrug off a heavy coat. 'It's just – I always wanted a dog.' He stared at her sadly for a moment. 'And Margaret's a great dog.' A spark came to his eye. 'Hey, I'm going to give it a go right now. Lil, pass me that ball.'

'This one?' Lil picked up Abe's 'thinker', a dirty tennis ball the colour of mould, which he used to throw against a wall while he was mulling things over. She carefully held it out for Nedly to take. He cradled it in his hands like an overripe peach, his eyes on it the whole time. 'Wait a minute; is this what you've been practising . . . ?'

'Shhhh,' said Nedly. 'I have to concentrate.'

Abe emerged from the bathroom, propped himself against the door frame and watched the ball move through the air.

'Nice trick,' he said. 'You know, if you could carry a ball with you all the time, then I'd know where you are.'

Nedly gasped. 'It takes quite a lot of effort

to carry a ball; I don't think I could do it for more than a few seconds.'

Lil reported back. 'No dice. Too much effort,' and then to Nedly she said, 'Don't tell me this is what you've been working on, all this time?' She could barely hide her disappointment. 'Flickering the lights, that weird hand thing and this?'

'Ha!' Nedly laughed and lost concentration, nearly dropping the ball. 'This is just the beginning. Just a second!' He took a deep breath, cried out, 'Here, Margaret!' and then let go. The ball bounced half-heartedly across the floor. Margaret didn't move.

Nedly took a step forward to retrieve it. Margaret's eyes widened, the whites showing, and she let out a low growl. Nedly took a step back. 'Lil! Pass me the ball again. I'm going to have another try; she wasn't ready.'

Lil gave Abe a look that held a deep and heavy sigh in it. 'I can't believe this is the other thing, Nedly.' As she retrieved the ball Margaret sprang up onto her back legs, tail wagging.

Lil threw the ball back at Nedly. It was too fast for him to catch but Margaret darted after it, snatched it from the ground when it bounced and walked off to bury it in her bed.

Nedly watched it vanish under the layers of blanket. 'Fetch,' he said weakly.

Lil took herself off to the bathroom before she said something she regretted. She stood, hands clutching the sink, looking into the cracked mirror. It was as though Nedly didn't want to learn anything useful. She ran the water until it faded from tea-coloured to beige and then splashed some on her face, patting it dry on the grey rag that passed as a towel.

She opened the door just in time to hear Abe saying, 'Margaret will come round, kid. Don't give up on her.' He was facing the wrong way again, but he still got a grateful smile out of Nedly.

Lil cleared her throat. 'So, are we leaving?'

Abe picked his hat off the stand, put it on and tugged the front brim down.

'I don't want to go to the morgue.' Nedly squirmed. 'It's full of dead people.'

Lil ignored him; she was too busy trying to stay hot on Abe's heels. So much so that when Abe opened the door she bowled into him.

Someone was standing right behind it.

Chapter 9

There's No Such Thing as Ghosts

'Absolom Mandrel?'

It was the man in the green poncho. Close up, Lil could see that the eyes behind the orange aviator specs were lively, his poncho was military issue and over one shoulder was slung a camo-print knapsack. He looked like he was ready for anything, except maybe the thing he was looking for.

Abe flicked up the brim of his hat. 'Who's asking?'

'My name is Irving Starkey and I am a –'

Abe cut across him, 'Sorry, pal. I was just on my way out. Care to make an appointment?'

Nedly ran to the appointment book and tried flicking the page over. Lil darted over to stop him and slammed the book shut.

'No appointment necessary.' She grinned brightly at him. 'We can spare a couple of minutes.'

If Starkey saw anything strange he didn't mention it, but he took the opportunity to take a step into the office and pulled off his hood, revealing a head that looked like it had been oiled and polished. The hood elastic had left a red ridge across his forehead, like his skull had been opened and then zipped shut again. 'I have one thing to ask you. It will only take a minute.'

He began a circuit around the room, pacing it out like one of those country-house detectives about to spill the juice on the murderer. He paused at Margaret and looked down at her with an awkward smile. Margaret returned the look without the smile.

'Who's this?

'That's my dog, Margaret.'

'Hmmm,' said Starkey. 'She's small for a dog.'

Abe sidled up, frowning. 'She's a small dog.'

'Yes, exactly,' he agreed enigmatically.

'She doesn't eat much and she's an expert at tailing someone without being seen. She can get into places too small for me and retrieve things, and she knows how to keep her mouth shut.'

'Curious name for a dog.'

'It was my mother's name,' Abe replied.

'Her tag says "Muffin", said Starkey, reading it.

Abe humphed. 'Well, I call her Margaret, and it's stuck now. She seems to like it anyway,' he added defensively. 'You didn't come here to talk about my dog, did you?'

'No.' Starkey turned his lively eyes on them. 'I came here to tell you that my name is Irving Starkey –' he paused dramatically – 'and I am a ghost hunter!'

Starkey looked at Abe, Abe looked at Lil, and Lil looked at Nedly, who backed into the corner, to the dark space behind the coat rack. The tension in the room was so thick you would have needed a pickaxe to break it up. Margaret didn't like it one bit and growled.

Lil ordered her eyes away from the coat rack and they found Abe's instead but in a split second his face became as still as an Easter Island statue. Lil tried to mimic it. She knew what the blank look meant; it was the equivalent of shutters being pulled down, nothing to be given away.

And so nobody moved.

Eventually, after seconds had passed and he'd worked out how to play it, Abe raised his eyebrows and said, 'You hunt ghosts?'

'I do.' Starkey pulled himself up to his full height, which was only slightly taller than Lil.

'You get enough work to make a living?' Abe asked conversationally.

'Actually, I'm retired. I used to be in insurance. But that's enough about me. I came here to tell you what I suspect you already know.' He began the pacing again. It was a small room and he had already done two circuits. Lil was starting to feel dizzy watching him and took up a perch on the corner of Abe's desk.

Starkey paused at the coat rack. 'There is a strange atmosphere in this room.' He let his eyes wander as though he was searching the air for invisible clues.

With a noise that only Lil could hear, like the whine as the last bit of air leaks out of a balloon, Nedly sank back through the wall. Lil could just make out the tip of his nose hovering there.

'Hmmm.' Starkey peeled one of Abe's damp socks off the broken radiator. 'The culprit, I think.' He gave Abe a discomforting look. 'I've heard stories, Detective Mandrel, on the streets. Stories of fear. Everyone is afraid but no one knows why.'

Lil flicked a glance at Nedly's nose. 'What stories?'

'Rumours, and more than rumours.' He took hold of the back of Abe's office chair as though he was going to give it a shoulder rub, and squeezed. 'People are vanishing under mysterious circumstances, and –' The chair shot away from him. Starkey fell to his knees behind the desk.

Lil rushed over. 'Are you OK?'

Starkey tried to brush it off but the pained expression on his face and the crack of his joints betrayed him.

He attempted to stand, treading on the hem of his poncho, which yanked him back to the floor face down. He clambered to his feet again, readjusted his glasses, hobbled round to the other side of the desk and sat down in the visitor's chair – somewhat defeated. This meeting clearly wasn't going as he had imagined.

Lil rescued Abe's chair from where it had skated, pulled it back to the desk and sat in it. Abe stood over her until she begrudgingly conceded the spot and went to perch on the arm of the leather settee instead.

Starkey cleared his throat and smoothed down the poncho. 'What was I . . . ? Ah yes. I believe that Peligan City is now the centre of an epidemic of spectral activity.' Abe frowned back at him. 'That is to say, it's haunted.'

'Ha, ha ha!' Abe broadcast a sudden mocking laugh. Lil tried to replicate it but she started too high and had to drop an octave to get the right level of derision.

'That's crazy,' she informed him.

Starkey whipped round to look at her with beady eyes. 'Is it? Perhaps you have heard the tale of Ramon LeTeef, the infamous gangster who had evaded capture, then handed himself in and was found to be quite mad – babbling stories of the revenge of long-dead associates?'

Abe stood up and strolled over to the window, prised apart the blades of the Venetian blind and looked out. 'Sounds like a great story; you should write it down.'

'Oh, I have. You see, I have a witness who claims that three months ago, when you apprehended LeTeef, you walked into a haunted house, terrorised by a type-1 spectral manifestation.'

'A what?'

'A spirit, detective. A ghost.' He let this word float around while the *drip, drip, drip* of melted snow trickled down the folds in his poncho, pooling on the floor around his chair in a donut-shaped puddle. 'A very powerful and frightening ghost. Right here, in Peligan City.

'And my witness told me that if I wanted to know more, Abe Mandrel was the man to talk to. You apprehended LeTeef,' he continued to Abe. 'I just want to know, what did you see?'

Lil reclaimed Abe's vacated chair and leant across the desk on both elbows. 'Who's your contact?'

Starkey looked uncomfortable. 'I have sworn to protect his identity.'

Lil gave Starkey the Penetrating Squint and he leant away from her as a low growl sounded in his ear and he turned to see Margaret sitting on the floor to his right. Abe completed the pincer movement, taking up position perched on the left-hand corner of the desk.

'So it's a man,' said Lil. 'Interesting.'

Starkey frowned at her and buttoned his lips.

They had him cornered; now it was time to turn the tables.

'What I'm wondering,' Lil said thoughtfully, 'is

how you even see ghosts to hunt them. I mean, they're invisible, aren't they?'

'Aha, the tricks of the trade! I have these glasses, for instance. They have special filters on them – I use them to identify patterns of electromagnetic energy –'

'Can I see them?' Lil held out her hand and Starkey reluctantly handed them over.

'I got them mail order,' he continued. 'Everyone should have a pair. And these are just the tip of the iceberg. I've seen equipment, experimental things . . .' He put his fingers to his mouth to stopper it.

They looked just like ordinary orange-tinted glass. Lil handed them back.

Starkey frowned at the spectacles, pulled the sleeve of a check shirt out from beneath his elasticated cuff and tried to shine Lil's thumbprint off one of the lenses. The lens popped out. Starkey bent down to pick it up and then knocked the back of his head on the corner of Abe's desk, tipping over the pencil pot in the process. Tears sprang into his eyes.

Lil dived in to help pick up the scattered pens and pocketed a couple. Starkey took a deep breath, returned to the chair, pushed the lens back into the frame and put the glasses on again. Nedly cautiously crept out from the wall space and started walking towards the ghost hunter.

'Stop!' hissed Lil.

Starkey looked up sharply. 'Stop what?'

'Stop fooling around,' Lil quickly explained. Nedly stood right in front of Starkey.

'Sorry, I-I'm –' the ghost hunter stammered. 'I'm a little accident-prone.' He looked offended. 'I don't do it on purpose.'

'He can't see me. The glasses don't work.' Nedly sounded disappointed. He leant right across the desk and waved one hand in front of Starkey's eyes. Lil could feel the hairs on the back of her neck begin to rise, but Starkey remained oblivious.

'He can't even feel me,' muttered Nedly to Lil. 'He's like your mum, totally immune.'

'Mr Mandrel.' Starkey blinked earnestly at Abe. 'I've spent my whole life in pursuit of proof that the spirits of the dead walk among us, but so far it has eluded me. Not so long ago I imagined ghosts to be lost and lonely souls whose lives had been snatched away – unable to leave the mortal world completely, they were stuck in limbo trying to right the wrongs that were done to them.'

Nedly's eyes met Lil's across the desk.

Starkey's voice hardened. 'But I have come to revise this opinion. Ghosts are not our friends. They can be unimaginably powerful and terrifying with a presence that goes way beyond cold spots and feelings of dread. We're talking advanced psychokinesis, electromagnetic interference and actual bodily harm. They must be stopped and I intend to stop them. With or without your assistance.' He got to his feet. 'Peligan City requires an exorcism!'

Abe clenched and unclenched his jaw. He breathed out loudly through his nose and then he said, 'Thanks all the same but I don't know what you're talking about. In my experience there's no such thing as ghosts.'

The orange rungs of the electric fire flared and then grew dull and the room became several degrees cooler. Nedly walked over to the window and stood in the glare of snow light.

Lil gave Abe a frown.

Starkey headed for the door. 'The people have a right to know what is happening.'

'Well, don't be surprised if they lock you up,' said Abe.

Starkey turned and gave Abe a look of bitter disappointment. 'I had hoped you would join us.'

'Who's us?'

Starkey squared up to Abe as much as he could and said with dignity, 'The Peligan City Paranormal Society. We are meeting later this morning.' He pulled the hood of his poncho back over his head. 'You should come along, detective. There will be biscuits.'

Abe tried to snort in a way that suggested he obviously wasn't the sort of person who could be lured in by biscuits.

'I could come?' volunteered Lil.

'It's not for children,' Starkey informed her. 'Ghosts are a serious business.'

'Right,' said Lil under her breath. 'What would I know?' She gave Nedly a look that said, 'You go, see what he's up to'. Nedly returned it with a nod that said, 'Leave it to me'.

Abe put his hand on the door as if he meant to close it, and preferably with Starkey on the other side. 'Well, this has all been very interesting, Mr Starkey, and I'm sorry I couldn't be more help, but it looks like someone has given you a bum steer.'

'So it seems,' Starkey replied cryptically. He patted Margaret on the head, saying, 'Goodbye, strange little dog.' Then he looked up at Abe. 'You know, people in this town have seen things that have turned their hair white. Just like that streak you have there under your hat.'

Abe smiled grimly. 'That's called getting old, pal.'

Starkey gave one last look around the room and walked out, his poncho flapping like a cape.

Once he was out of earshot Abe muttered, 'What a crackpot!'

Lil bit on her lip. 'He was right, though, wasn't he? Peligan City *is* haunted.'

They stood in the doorway, listening to Starkey's tread on the stairs. A strangled-sounding yelp told them he had reached the rotten board on the second-to-last stair. Finally the click of the door opening and the bang of it shutting behind him meant they were alone.

Abe turned back to the office. 'Hey, Nedly. What I said about not believing in ghosts – you know I didn't mean it, right?'

'Forget it,' said Lil, giving him a hard stare. 'He's gone.'

Chapter 10

Peligan City Morgue

The snow followed the patterns of the wind as it blew around the city, twisting and swerving past street lamps, buffeting cars and freezing all those who were unlucky enough to be walking through it.

Abe and Lil left the car a block away and Margaret stayed behind to guard it, nestled in a Mexican rug with 'Classical Hour' on the radio and a strip of rawhide to keep her company.

Peligan City Morgue was located on a back street, round the corner from the hospital.

Abe rang the buzzer on the intercom. There was a click as someone picked up.

'It's me.' Abe waited for the muffled reply and then elaborated. 'Me, Abe Mandrel. Monbatsu said we could swing by, take a look at . . .' He shrugged at Lil – neither knew exactly what Monbatsu wanted to show them so Abe went for the obvious. 'A stiff.'

A long pause followed.

'Look,' Abe persevered, 'it's snowing cats and dogs out here – will you let us in?' The buzzer sounded and the lock released.

They walked down the stairs to a cold basement area. The morgue technician, whose name badge said 'Edmund Cloake' met them at the bottom. He had the complexion of uncooked pastry and a large, pointed Adam's apple. His dark hair was parted in the middle and hung down to his shoulders. He wore fingerless gloves and a tatty grey-and-red striped scarf over his lab coat.

He narrowed his eyes when he saw Lil. 'Who's the kid?'

'I'm his partner,' Lil replied.

'Sidekick,' Abe corrected.

'Associate,' Lil conceded

Cloake frowned. 'I heard you had a dog now?'

'I'm his other associate,' said Lil through gritted teeth.

Cloake led them into a long concrete corridor punctuated with dingy lights that hummed overhead. The air smelt cold and sterile with a sweet undercurrent of death that clung to the back of their throats. Closed doors with small metal plaques informed them that they were passing the laboratory, the autopsy room, the instrument sterilisation room and the cold storage until finally they reached the chief pathologist's office.

Monbatsu was waiting for them. 'Ah, Mandrel! Nice of you to drop by unexpectedly.' He nodded Cloake away. 'That will be all, thank you.'

Cloake narrowed his eyes again. 'He said he was here to see a stiff.'

'Ha!' Monbastu smiled wryly. 'I think he was talking about me. Now, there is still some testing to be done on 367, Cloake. Don't let us detain you any longer.'

Cloake hesitated, his Adam's apple sliding up and down a couple of times, then he left them to it.

Before anyone could speak Monbatsu had closed the door and then moved quickly towards a transistor radio that sat on top of a filing cabinet and switched it on. Piano music of the classical type filled the room.

'So if you're looking for the unusual, Mandrel, I have an embarrassment of riches.'

Lil took her notebook out of her back pocket and flicked it open at the next blank page. She pulled out a pencil, twirled it once and it spun off and rolled under one of Monbatsu's cabinets. She sighed inwardly. 'I'm just going to borrow this.' She reached across and took a pen off the desk.

Monbatsu raised an eyebrow. 'Our conversation will be off the record, I hope.'

'Naturally.' Lil smiled wolfishly at him, mentally punching the air at being party to an actual off-the-record conversation.

'Very well. I do have a particular matter I would like to draw your attention to but first –' he typed a number into the keypad on the cabinet, opened a drawer and pulled out two pink cardboard files – 'take a look at this.' He passed the first one to Abe. 'I finished the Minos autopsy yesterday afternoon. Most interesting.'

Abe opened the file, took a look and blanched, slamming it shut and thwarting Lil's attempt to see it for herself.

'He's been crushed to a pulp,' said Monbatsu. 'Every bone. It's the sort of fracture you see when a body gets caught up in heavy machinery, and yet I do not believe this was the work of a machine.'

'You think a person did it?' There was a lull in the music and in it another sound, like someone's weight shifting against a door.

Monbatsu looked up sharply. He got to his

feet and started walking very softly towards the door. 'Hmmm, yes, I think so.'

He opened the door suddenly and Cloake fell through it.

'Ha! There you are. Very conveniently. Cloake, my coffee machine is out of order. Here.' He reached into his pocket and pulled out three banknotes. 'Fetch us some from the cafe round the corner, please.'

Monbatsu watched Cloake put on his coat and hat and then disappear up the corridor, before continuing, 'Where was I? Ah yes, Minos. His bones weren't snapped quickly, like a breadstick. They were squeezed.'

'So,' said Abe, loosening his collar, 'the perp would have to have been strong to kill someone in this way?'

'Extremely,' Monbatsu agreed. 'The last time I saw injuries like this was back in Morris Hoxon's day.' He turned to Lil. 'Hoxon, known as the Minotaur due to his disproportionately large head and shoulders. He was, as they say, a "heavy", a hired hand. He used to rough people up, put "the frighteners" on them.' Monbatsu spoke without emotion. 'The shoulders of an ox, arms like boa constrictors; he was most certainly capable of crushing a man to death.'

'I've heard of him,' said Abe. 'He's been locked up in the Needle for the last thirty years.'

Monbatsu shook his head grimly.

'They released him?'

Monbatsu shook his head again.

'You think he's been sprung?' Lil looked up from her note-taking long enough to widen her eyes and then she narrowed them again. 'Wouldn't he be a bit old for these kind of moves now?'

'Hoxon Morris died a couple of weeks ago. Whatever this epidemic is, it killed him.'

'Hmmmm.' Abe stroked his chin thoughtfully then, finding a large patch he had missed while he was shaving, stopped drawing attention to it. 'What's in the other file?'

'This came in early this morning. There are similarities. Let me show you.'

Abe waved the offer away like it was a bowl of cold sick. 'That's OK.'

Monbatsu smiled and opened the file to him anyway. 'Look at the picture.' He held it out to Abe but Lil was faster; she took in a long look, saw what appeared to be an unwrapped mummy with parched and wrinkled skin, and grimaced.

Abe peered at it from the corner of his eye and then looked closer. 'Where did they find that, a museum?'

Monbatsu looked at the picture himself and then held it up. 'How old would you say this woman was?'

Lil gave what she hoped was an appraising look before guessing. 'Fifty?'

Abe snorted. 'More like a hundred.'

Monbatsu frowned. 'She's actually in her thirties.'

'Who was she?' asked Lil.

'Sal Xu Ping, proprietor of five of the seven casinos in the Golden Loop. She was poisoned.'

Abe grimaced at the image. 'What kind of poison would do that to a person?'

'A very specific one, very complex – the toxicology report was two pages long. And here, once again, you benefit from my considerable years of experience, for I have known of this particular complex of drugs before. Many years ago this exact concoction was the calling card of Peligan City's most notorious poisoner, Blackheath Carrick.'

'I don't know the guy,' said Abe.

'No. It would have been before your time, detective. I was a medical student back then and I remember studying the case.'

'So did the fuzz pick him up?'

'After a time. He's been incarcerated ever since.'

'Until . . . ?' Lil paused, her pen hovering over the notebook.

Monbatsu shrugged. 'Until forever. As far as I know he's still in the Needle. So you see, Mandrel, you have two bodies, both murdered in ways known to be the *modus operandi* of criminals of a bygone age, one of whom is a very old man now and one of whom is deceased.

'And that's not all, I've gone back over the files for the last few months and there were five other mysterious deaths recorded as either misadventure or natural causes. All high-profile people, all with unsavoury connections.'

'Are we looking at a copycat?'

'You're the detective.'

'What would be the motive?'

'For replicating the M.O. of these notorious criminals? Not a clue. Fame perhaps? A little notoriety by association? Ask a behavioural scientist. But the motivation behind his choice of victims?' Monbatsu took up a perch on the corner of his desk and eyed them levelly. 'If I was a gambling man, which I am, I would bet on a coup in the making – someone is moving into position to take control of Peligan by knocking out all the big players.

'And another thing, remember the Firebug Killer? He came after you once, Mandrel, didn't he?'

Here comes the connection. Lil knew it. She waited, not even breathing; her gaze snuck its way over to Abe. He gave Monbatsu a stiff-shouldered shrug as he said, 'What of it?'

'I couldn't help drawing a comparison. You

see, just like Minos, Ping and the others, there was never any investigation into his crimes, because there were never any clues, just the bodies. No witnesses, no fingerprints. Nothing. The Firebug did the police a favour when he stopped; they never would have caught him – he was too clever.' Monbatsu looked out of his window at the brick wall just beyond, as though he was trying to read something in the pattern of the mortar. 'There's something about his crimes and these that worries me.' Then he snapped out of it in a hurry. 'Which brings me to the real reason I asked you here today.'

There was more? Lil's pen was poised at the ready.

Monbatsu continued, 'These cases I've shown you are just the headline grabbers.'

'Which have so far failed to grab any headlines,' said Lil.

'Indeed.' Monbatsu paused. He checked the door again and lowered his voice to a whisper. 'I have in my possession a set of reports, which I am calling the Fright File. It proves that we are in the midst of something truly terrifying. The death rate in Peligan City has octupled over the last month.'

Lil gasped. 'Murder?'

'Officially they are being recorded as death by exposure. All of the victims bar one had been living on the streets. Of course, the death rate is always high this time of year, especially now, since City Hall closed most of the shelters – it's the cold. But these people didn't die of exposure.'

'How do you know?'

He tapped the plastic badge on his lapel. 'Because I am a forensic pathologist. Exposure is a long, slow death; this was fast – seconds, I would say. I don't know why the cause of their deaths are being misdiagnosed but it's very strange, because all the victims had the same three superficial things in common. They all died relatively instantly, they all bore expressions resembling a rictus, and their hair had all turned to white at the time of death.

'I have now had a chance to examine one of

these misdiagnosed bodies closely and my findings indicate that the victim died of sudden heart failure,' Monbatsu explained, his eyes never leaving Abe's. 'Now, I don't like to make guesses, but if I was to make a guess, and when I say guess, I mean an informed medical judgement based on forty years as an expert in the field . . . I'd say she was scared to death.'

Lil and Abe exchanged foreboding glances, and Abe asked, 'Why haven't we heard anything about this until now?'

'That's the question I've been asking myself.'

Lil's eyes widened. 'Hushed up?' She folded her arms cynically. 'But you haven't told anyone either.'

'Oh, but I have,' Monbatsu replied, offended. 'I went right to the top.'

'Acting Mayor Gordian?' Abe guessed. 'What did she say?'

Monbatsu shook his head and shrugged. 'I'm still waiting for someone to come and start investigating. So far no one has.'

Lil took an involuntary step back and trod

on Abe's foot. 'Sorry! So, have you I.D.d any of the bodies?'

'Some of them.'

'So –' she raised her Cryptic Eyebrow – 'who was the one?'

'I'm sorry?'

Lil read back through her notes. 'You said "all bar one had been living on the streets". Who is the exception?'

'Minos's driver,' replied Monbatsu, giving Lil an admiring nod. 'Until yesterday morning, the copycat murders and these cases in the Fright File appeared completely unconnected.'

Abe tried to muscle in on the brain action with a quick recap. 'So, Minos is killed in a method known to be that of a deceased criminal and the only potential witness appears to have died of fright at the scene?'

'That's about the size of it,' Monbatsu concluded.

'And,' Abe continued, 'as the cause of death appears to be the same as several others, you think maybe they saw something too. Something that frightened them so much it killed them?'

Lil flashed her eyes at him. A ghost. One that was capable of killing by fear alone. This was it. The lead they had been waiting for. Gallows had been terrorising Peligan City for a while but for some reason it had been hushed up, and who knows how many people had died in the meantime. A sudden, horrible thought crept into Lil's mind.

'The woman you examined. Do you know who she was?'

'I call her 362.' Monbatsu shrugged. 'She was a rough sleeper. I thought she looked familiar. Maybe I'd seen her before somewhere but I couldn't make an I.D.'

'There's someone I'm looking for. A woman. She has been missing for days now. Can you check in the file? See if she's there?'

Monbastu returned to the filing cabinet and began flicking through the folders within. The file wasn't in the cabinet. He searched the papers on his benches, and patted down the pockets of the duffle coat that was hanging on a hook on the wall. 'I know I had it last night.' He hefted his brown-leather doctor's bag onto the table and frantically rummaged through. 'It's not here. Someone has stolen it!'

Abe flexed his steely jaw. 'Was that your only proof?'

Monbatsu sighed. 'I still have the victim I examined. 362. She's in the cold storage now.'

Lil couldn't bear the not knowing. She couldn't wait any longer. Without a word she darted from the office, down the murky corridor to the room labelled 'Cold Storage' and shoved the door open. She could hear Abe calling her name, hurrying after her, but she ignored him. Racing to the wall of metal cabinets she scanned through until she found it, number 362, and with all her might she pulled the drawer open and looked down before she could stop herself.

She would never be able to forget what she saw there: lips that were stretched and blue, pulled back over brown teeth. Eyes open wide, the yellowish tinge standing out against powdery skin. The fingers were raised and bent like claws clutching at the air, and hair that streamed back from a thin face, as fuzzy and white as snow. It was Delilah. Lil had found her at last.

Chapter 11

The Peligan City
Paranormal Society

The lunch-hour crowd was just finishing up and drifting away by the time Lil, Abe and Margaret arrived at the Nite Jar Cafe. As atmospheres went it was as far from the morgue as you could get; the juke box was belting out ragtime jazz and the air was warm and smelt of ground coffee and sweet pastries.

They took a corner booth at the far end, and peeled off their frosted macs. Abe dumped his on the chair beside him and Lil hung hers over the back of the seat. Velma came over with her notebook to get their order.

Abe squinted at the baked goods in the glass display domes along the counter. 'Can I get a sausage roll, two apple Danish –' He gave Lil a querying look and saw her shake her head in reply. 'One apple Danish,' he revised the order, 'and a cup of java, please.'

'Sure.' Velma worked her jaws around the gum she was chewing. 'What will it be for you, Lil?'

'Just a glass of water, please.'

Velma held her fingers, tipped with frosted pink varnish, softly against Lil's brow. 'Are you OK, honey? You're as white as a sheet.'

Lil nodded and gulped.

'She's had a shock,' Abe explained.

Velma gave him a look. 'What kind of shock?'

Abe raised his shoulders, preparing to explain but then realising mid-gesture that the truth would sound worse than anything Velma could imagine, then let them drop with a defeated sigh. 'A pretty bad one, but she'll be OK.'

Velma returned a moment later with their order.

As soon as they were alone again Lil let her head drop into her hands. 'I'm so embarrassed.'

Abe crinkled his eyes at her. 'Don't be hard on yourself. No kid should see something like that, no matter how tough they are.' He began dismantling the sausage roll and alternately eating bits and dropping bits onto the floor for Margaret. 'I've known plenty of hard nuts crack up when they see their first dead body.' He gave Lil a concerned look. 'You knew her?'

Lil nodded. She couldn't seem to talk.

Abe continued, 'I knew her a bit myself, back in the day; she used to be a singer in the Two Deuces. Fell on hard times, harder than most.' Lil nodded again. 'There was an article about her in the *Klaxon* recently.'

'I know,' Lil began and then faltered. 'I – I read it.'

They sat in silence for a few minutes while Abe chewed on the sausage roll and Lil stared out of the window. Then he pushed his empty plate away and knocked back the last of the roll with a glug of coffee. 'So, Monbatsu's copycat theory – what did you make of all that?'

Lil chewed her lip thoughtfully. 'You know that second prisoner he mentioned, the poisoner, Carrick? I'm pretty sure he's dead too. A couple of days ago. Another victim of the epidemic at the Needle.'

'Well, he must have been in his nineties so I'm not surprised he got sick.'

'That's two dead criminals with very specific M.O.s followed by two crimes with their exact hallmark. I don't think it is a copycat.' Lil leant across the table. 'I think those criminals have been sprung. Sprung into the afterlife, and if I'm right and it's their ghosts we're dealing with, then I'll bet Gallows is behind it.'

Abe looked at Lil and she stared right back. 'Maybe,' he said.

'When Nedly gets back from tailing Starkey we're going to head over to the library and do some digging. Find out who exactly has died and when.'

'Are you sure you feel up to it?'

Lil swallowed hard and nodded. 'What are you going to do?'

Abe found a crumb on the table and stared at it. 'Well, I've got to meet Naomi in an hour, so . . .'

'Fine, leave all the investigating to me and Nedly. We'll let you know.'

From below the table they heard a low growling noise. Then, with a sound that only Lil could hear, like a zip being pulled, a flickering of the overhead lamp and a slight feeling of dread, Nedly materialised beside her. Lil scooted away from him, towards the window, her heartbeat racing a little.

'Sorry!' Nedly was taken aback at her unusually wan face. 'Are you OK? Did I scare you?'

'Yes. No.' She paused to take a sip of water and shook her head. 'It's not you.'

Abe got the measure of the conversation, glanced around and then with one hand over his mouth he explained, 'She's had a shock,' to the space beside Lil.

'Can you stop telling everyone that?' Lil snapped. 'I'm fine now. Even a tough nut can crack up.'

'Right,' Nedly agreed uncertainly.

Lil stuck her fists in her eye sockets and gave them a rub. 'It was Delilah. She's dead!'

She looked up, blinking, and saw Nedly's face as it fell.

'Dead?'

Lil nodded. 'And she's not the only one . . . You should have seen her . . .' She went green around the gills as the memory flooded back. 'I don't want to talk about it.'

Nedly looked relieved. 'I don't want you to talk about it.'

'It was horrible,' Lil continued. 'She was lying there, her face –'

'Please don't talk about it.'

Lil stared into the glass and her own disturbingly rippled face looked back at her. 'I can't help it; it's all I can think about.'

Abe tapped the table with his rubber hand. 'You can fill Nedly in on the morgue later, when you've got your shine back. Now, how about we change the subject?' He fixed his gaze more or less on where Lil had been looking, and cupped his other hand over his mouth again. 'Nedly, how did you get on?'

Lil tucked her hair behind her ears and took a deep breath. 'Right. Of course. The Paranormal Society, sorry, Nedly.' She grabbed her notebook and pencil from her rucksack and settled down to business. 'OK, ready when you are.'

Nedly leant across the table, conspiratorially; Lil leant forward too while Abe tried to casually retreat, away from the incoming creeps. Margaret took the opportunity to nip the edge of Abe's mac between her little teeth and pull it onto the floor where she made a nest in it.

'So,' Nedly began slowly, 'I followed him to this club called the Masonic Rooms, down on the west side, by that old swimming pool. They had only just opened up and the man behind the bar was wiping down the tables and shining up the glasses.'

Lil echoed his every word, relaying the story

to Abe but with a lot less expression because she was busy writing too.

'The barman seemed to know Starkey and gave him a sympathetic nod when he walked in. He took a pew at the table beside the juke box. It was playing a kind of . . .' He lost confidence in this line when he saw Abe's gaze drift down to the apple Danish. 'So, anyway, he pulled out a paper plate and a packet of biscuits –'

Lil cut in. 'What kind of biscuits?'

'Is that important?' Abe frowned at her.

'It might be.'

'They were custard creams, I think.'

'Custard creams.' Lil raised the Cryptic Eyebrow. 'Value pack?'

'No, one of the small ones. And before he laid them on the table he opened the top.'

'But didn't shake them out onto the plate?'

'No, he just left them on the table like that.'

Abe knocked back the last of his coffee. 'I appreciate the detail, kid, but get to the point.'

Nedly sat back awkwardly. 'Sorry.'

'He's just setting the scene,' Lil said defensively.

'It's his first real report; who knows what kind of information will be important at this stage?'

She glanced over her notes. 'So far, from the intel that Nedly has collected we know that Starkey doesn't have much money: custard creams are the cheapest of the fancy biscuits, and you don't get many in a packet so he wasn't expecting lots of people, but maybe he was expecting at least one, and he wanted to make them welcome. Although he wasn't entirely sure they were definitely going to show, because he didn't shake them out of the packet.'

Nedly was staring at Lil with a look of amazement.

'Don't you think?' She raised her eyebrows.

For a moment he didn't say anything at all but then he cleared his throat and said, 'Yep, exactly that.'

Lil smiled encouragingly. 'Go on, then what happened?'

Nedly leant in again. 'Well, nothing for thirty minutes. Every time the door opened he looked up hopefully, but otherwise he just sat there

149

nursing a glass of ginger ale, which the barman gave him, on the house – I think he felt sorry for him and he said something like, "No show again, Irving?" and Starkey offered him a biscuit. But the barman didn't take one. I think I might have accidentally given him the creeps.'

Lil nodded. Abe sighed.

'But maybe he just didn't like custard creams. Anyway,' Nedly added quickly, trying to speed up, 'so nothing happened again for a bit.'

'So it was a waste of time then?' Abe suggested.

'No, one thing did happen. At ten to eleven, when Starkey had been sitting there for almost an hour, guess who walked in?'

Lil's eyes widened. 'Cornelius Gallows?'

'What!' Abe sat up suddenly.

'Sorry, no, that was my guess. He said, "Guess who walked in?"'

Abe huffed with impatience.

'Gordian?' Lil tried again.

Abe's fuse was growing shorter by the minute. 'Was that another guess?'

'Yes,' Lil replied to Abe.

'No,' Nedly told Lil.

Abe clenched and unclenched his jaw again. 'Can't he just say who it is without you guessing?'

'It was Craig Weasel!' Nedly blurted out. 'Mayor Dean's old bodyguard!'

Lil let her jaw drop then she shook her head in a scandalised way and wrote it down.

'Who was it?' Abe asked eagerly, trying to decipher Lil's scribble upside down.

She let him stew for a minute and then put down her pencil and told him. Abe trawled back through his memories. 'The pea-head with the red hair and the silk pyjamas?'

Nedly nodded. 'The very same – only now his hair is snowy white.'

Lil thought for a moment. 'Weasel must be Starkey's source; he was there that night when we apprehended LeTeef. He must have known that the house was haunted. I bet he got spooked and that's why he ran, and lived to tell the tale. So, what did they talk about?'

Nedly looked uncomfortable. 'That I don't

exactly know. The thing was, Starkey isn't sensitive to me at all so I could sit with him, no problem, but Weasel was a different story. He had the creeps straight away; he got really twitchy and he wouldn't sit down. Starkey tried to reassure him, even offered to lend him his glasses, but Weasel wasn't having any of it – so I had to move away a bit and watch them from afar.'

'And?'

'Well, they talked for a while, but I couldn't hear what they were saying.' Lil gave Nedly a disapproving look. 'I couldn't help it! But I did see one more thing – Weasel gave Starkey a folder.'

'What kind of folder?'

Nedly shrugged. 'Cardboard, I think.' Lil let her head drop back and sighed. 'But when Starkey opened it his eyes went really wide and he started sweating. I know that because I saw him mop his head with the serviette from his drink. He nodded at Weasel and then he grabbed the folder really tightly in his fist, so his knuckles were almost white – like he'd really got hold of something.'

'What was in the folder?'

'Paper of some kind, I think. I wish I knew what was written on it. Something important, I'll bet,' he added earnestly.

Lil gritted her teeth in an effort not to say '*obviously*'. 'So, once Starkey had the information in the folder, whatever it was, where did he go next?'

'I don't know,' Nedly said, 'because I came straight here to tell you about Weasel and the folder.'

Lil took a deep breath and then relayed the information to Abe in her most neutral voice. Abe squeezed the apple Danish he was about to take a bite out of so tightly that some of the filling oozed out and hit the table with a plop. In a flash of fur Margaret leapt, sucked it up and then disappeared again.

'OK, well,' Lil said. 'Good work – for the most part. We'll just have to see how this plays out now.'

Abe rubbed his jaw pensively. 'We better keep an eye on this Starkey character. They say a little knowledge is a dangerous thing.'

Nedly frowned. 'I feel sorry for him. He wants so badly to know that ghosts are real.'

He stared out of the window, at the large flakes of snow that were falling past.

Lil looked too, though hers was the only reflection she saw in the glass.

Chapter 12

Jailbreak

The reading room of the Peligan City Library was empty as usual but Lil still made a furtive survey of the space as she crossed the great wheel of book shelves to the librarian's desk and gathered up a stack of index-card boxes.

'I think I'll take all of these down with us,' she told Nedly. 'We don't know what the best search will be and we can't waste time going up and down.' She took off her mac and covered the boxes with it.

Nedly cast an anxious glance at the closed door of the librarian's office. 'You're not supposed to take those out of the reading room. What if someone else needs them?'

Lil high-tailed it to the service lift with Nedly jogging in her wake. 'I know, but I think this is some kind of emergency, and there's no one around to ask so . . .' She shrugged, yanked the grille across and punched the 'down' button to take them to the basement.

When they reached the bottom Lil turned the override key to 'off' to prevent anyone coming down after them. 'No interruptions. We need the skinny on these spooks ASAP, if that's what they are.'

Unlike the library, the basement – a large windowless vault with a concrete floor – had always been closed to the public. The stacks that furnished it were dusty and dark and their shelves groaned with newspapers: Peligan's recorded history in decades of newsprint, all the back copies of the *Herald* and the *Chronicle* there had ever been. If the *Klaxon* was down there too, Lil had never found it, but then the *Klaxon* was contraband: if there was an archive, it would have to be a secret one. Lil's mind went fleetingly to the office upstairs.

The dim lighting, consisting of old yellowed tubes running along the ceiling, was only brightened in the reading area, where a pendant lamp with its own pull cord dangled over an unvarnished ply table and a couple of metal chairs. Lil switched on an electric fire, which radiated nothing but the smell of burning dust, placed the index boxes on the table and flexed her knuckles.

She felt a peculiar thrill; it was the beginning of something, the first free strand in the untangling of a web. She took a deep breath of air that smelt of mothballs and old newsprint, coughed a few times and then rolled up her sleeves.

'OK.' She looked at Nedly. 'Let's get to it. I'll retrieve the papers, you find the articles.' The key to their story was down there somewhere, hidden amongst the shelves in boxes and piles, and with the index file to guide her, Lil was going to shake the secrets from the dusty Archives and make a case so watertight that not even the *Herald* could spin it.

'We know at least two names, Morris and Carrick – we'll work from there.' Lil rifled through the index until she found the ticket for Morris, Hoxon. There were just three mentions: his arrest, his trial and then, only a few weeks ago, his death.

The newspapers were kept in archive boxes, one for each month. The boxes were lined up on rolling stacks: bays of shelving on a wheeled traction system. At the end of each bay was a turning handle, like a go-cart steering wheel, which propelled the bays along the tracks, opening and closing the stacks wherever access to the shelves was needed.

For a few minutes there was silence but for the soft whirr of revolving wheels followed by the sound of Lil rifling through boxes. She laid each paper in front of Nedly with the index card and he applied himself to trying to flip the pages until he found the story.

Morris Hoxton looked like a cartoon. He had a huge upper body balanced on thin hips and small delicate feet. A massive jaw, ox-like shoulders, barely any neck, fists like sledgehammers. He was known to have crushed bones with his bare hands, but could his ghost really have been behind Minos's death?

Blackheath Carrick was next: a former Peligan City chemist and its most infamous poisoner. He had remained undetected for years; it wasn't established how many deaths he had been responsible for before he was caught. There was a shot of him that looked like it had been taken at a portrait studio. A slight man, grey thinning hair combed back from his forehead in oily lines, large front teeth and a weak chin. He had been jailed for life, and had served almost fifty years before he died.

Lil jotted down the dates with a frown. 'According to the *Herald*, Carrick died only a few days ago. If he did kill Ping he must have literally gone out and committed a signature murder straight after. You know what that

159

means?' She gave Nedly a grave look. 'Gallows is speeding up; it took him nearly a year to train Mr Glimmer, now he's turning them out almost overnight. Mass production.'

Nedly nodded. 'Yes, but Leonard Owl was no killer, whereas Carrick and Morris . . . He's just asking them to do what they've done before.'

'Hmmm,' Lil mused. 'You know what I'm wondering?' She propped her head on her hand and turned it to face Nedly. 'I'm wondering if there even is an epidemic. I mean, it's all very convenient, Gallows somehow getting to them just at the point of death and weaponising their ghosts. How does he even know when to show up? Unless he's the one who decides who gets sick in the first place.

'I think the epidemic is a smoke screen – Gallows has found a way to execute the ones he wants, and a way to cover it up.' She sighed through her nose. 'We've just got to figure out how he's doing it.'

She thought it over for a moment and then

shook her attention back to the task in hand and tapped the index box. 'Right, let's see who else. Monbatsu only recognised the M.O. in two of the cases. There might be more.'

She found the card for the prison and scanned down to where it was cross-referenced with the word 'death'. There were lots of entries but in the last few months only six.

Sawney Argo had been imprisoned for blackmail and extortion ten years earlier. They hadn't been able to prove it in court but he was also implicated in the suicides of the victims he was blackmailing. It had never been ascertained whether his victims had killed themselves because they were being blackmailed or he had killed them when they couldn't or wouldn't pay up.

Lil stopped chewing her pencil and tapped the article with it. 'I'd be willing to bet that he took out Silverman.'

Grima Cadiz, aka the Grey Hood, was a former stenographer at the Peligan City courthouse who started dealing out her own justice to those who had escaped confinement. She was known for drugging and drowning people in the river. There was no picture of her but there was a drawing from a witness I.D. that showed a woman in a hood.

'Urgh!' Lil shuddered. 'She's the creepiest of them all. And her M.O. is death by drowning. I wonder how many people have been fished out of the Kowpye lately. If she was behind any of them, there wouldn't be any way of knowing now.'

That made two possibles and two certainties, but Lil knew that people died in prison all the time; they wouldn't have made the papers unless they were infamous.

Nevertheless there was one other candidate, a notable death that had been recorded weeks before the epidemic was given that name.

It should have made big news, because the prisoner was the most notorious killer that Peligan City had ever known, but he was old and his death was not unexpected. It had been buried in the back pages, amongst the notices.

It was a credit to the eagle eyes of the librarian that it had been caught and indexed at all, so that Lil found it in her search: four months earlier, while Mr Glimmer, the ghost of Leonard Owl, had been setting light to Gallows' old enemies, a prisoner had died. His name was Loid Grainne and he was known as the Peligan City Strangler.

Lil shivered. 'Nedly,' she murmured quietly. 'I think I've found the first one.'

Nedly shivered and a ripple of unease spread through the basement. The naked bulb overhead swayed slightly, pulling and squashing Lil's shadow across the table while around them the air grew cold. Lil slipped her mac back on.

The article had been published six months earlier, just as a notice in the ads near the back:

Peligan City Strangler Dies in Prison
Grainne was seventy years old. His reign of terror lasted three years. He was incarcerated for twelve consecutive life sentences and had served forty-four years at the time of his death.

Lil frowned at Nedly and reached for the card index. She found a reference from around the time of the trial, and then several more using the search term 'Peligan City Strangler'. He was obviously big news back in the day.

Lil thumbed her way to the pages on Loid Grainne's arrest. There was a picture, an artist's impression that the police had used for his 'wanted' poster.

Grainne had large round glassy eyes, so dark they appeared black in the greyscale portrait and a thin slash mouth. Plastered-down hair, sharp black eyebrows and a flat white face. There was something terrifying about his expression. He looked like a grave-faced Pierrot. The sight of him made Lil's skin crawl.

'Mr Grip,' Nedly whispered.

Lil closed the paper carefully and folded it and then put it in the nearest box and squashed down the lid with both hands. 'I wish I hadn't seen him.'

'Me too.' Nedly blanched queasily.

Chapter 13

The Brave Dr Lankin

The last death they found was the most recent, that of Balthazar Minos. As far as Lil could tell it was the only one that occurred outside the Secure Wing, but then Minos was a victim not a perpetrator. There was a picture of the steel-hearted former governor standing at the foot of the Needle during the press conference he gave after the apparent suicide of Dr Hans Carvel. Minos had a white buzz cut and a thick moustache that obscured his top lip. He was squat and solid and someone, or something, had crushed him to a pulp.

Nedly looked sadly at the photograph. 'Do you think he was killed because he found out what Gallows was up to, that the epidemic was a fake?'

Lil shrugged. 'Maybe he was about to spill the beans?' The caption below the photograph read 'Governor Minos welcomes Carvel's replacement, Dr Alector Lankin'.

Lankin was standing well behind Minos, modestly shying away from the limelight. 'Those prisoners were all safely locked up in the Secure Wing, but Gallows still managed to get at them. Do you think we should warn Dr Lankin? He's trapped in there too.'

'I'm surprised he's still around.' Nedly frowned. 'I would have thought he would have been on Gallows' list too. He used to work with Carvel at Rorschach. It was Lankin's observations that Carvel recorded in Gallows' psychiatric report, remember?' He leant over to study the photograph.

Lil grasped the edge of the table excitedly. 'Maybe he's in league with Gallows, maybe that's how he's getting to the prisoners. Maybe they've always been in league with each other? It would explain a lot.

'I mean, it can't be easy for Gallows to get into the prison without some reason for visiting and now that the epidemic has been declared it must be almost impossible. He must have someone on the inside!'

'He does,' said Nedly, his eyes hardening.

'Exactly!' Lil exclaimed and then she added, 'What do you mean?'

Nedly pursed his lips. 'Look up Lankin on the cards.'

'He's right there.' She prodded the photograph.

'No, find an earlier one. See if there's one from before the asylum burnt down.'

Lil found Lankin's name in the files and then rolled back the stack to retrieve a copy of the *Chronicle* from fifteen years earlier, it had been taken when the young doctor, Alector Lankin, had first started work at Rorschach. In the picture he was standing with his colleague, Hans Carvel, both were wearing bow ties and grins with their lab coats. Lankin's coat was undone and a generous belly swelled over the cinch of his trousers. In between his curly hair and his beard he wore thick framed glasses and had rosy apple cheeks.

'Spot the difference,' said Nedly.

Lil held the pictures up against each other. Even at a distance she could see that the Dr Lankin in the later photograph was older, naturally, and he was a lot thinner too; the years hadn't been kind and his once amiable face was gaunt and sallow-looking. But there was something else . . . It was difficult to tell with the differences of scale, but if she had to guess, Lil would also have said he had grown about fifteen centimetres taller.

'They're not the same man.'

She took the magnifying glass out of her rucksack and used it to peer more closely at the later picture. The image spread out beneath the lens, until it was just a pattern of dots, but something about the formation was familiar. Lil drew back, dropping the glass as finally she saw what Nedly had seen. Between Lankin's dark curly hair and full beard his eyes were sunken and colourless. Eyes they had seen before.

Nedly nodded grimly. 'The first photograph is Alector Lankin, former psychiatrist at Rorschach Asylum and the second photograph is Cornelius Gallows, former patient, pretending to be Lankin.'

Lil flumped back in her chair, exclaiming, 'So that's where he went!' Then she sat forward again. 'So, if he's in there, where's Lankin?'

Nedly gave an open-handed shrug. 'Maybe he didn't survive the original fire? Gallows said he stole a dead doctor's lab coat to make his escape. Maybe it was Lankin's?'

'Good point.' Lil rubbed her fingertips against her temples in small circles, thinking hard. 'So we know how Gallows got in. How is he getting out, past the quarantine?'

'He doesn't need to; he can send the ghosts out from there. What's more, as long as he's

169

behind bars and the epidemic is going on, no one can touch him. He's completely safe.'

Lil gave her pencil a thoughtful twirl. 'So, if our theory is correct and, as Monbatsu said, the cases are connected, then, unlike the Firebug, there were witnesses to these spook attacks – lots of them, only none of them lived to tell the tale; they all ended up in the Fright File!'

Lil switched on the photocopier and waited while it shunted to life. 'Even without the ghosts, what we have here is an evil genius back from the dead masquerading as a prison doctor and then faking an epidemic so he can murder the prisoners in his care. Nedly, this is going to be bigger than the exposé on City Hall. This is going to be the scoop of the year.'

She began haphazardly photocopying the newspaper articles, throwing the pages face-down onto the glass top while the green scanning light paced back and forth across the surface. Discarded papers piled up as the copier spewed out duplicates on the other side.

Lil and Nedly stood together, looking down at the pile of evidence at their feet. The grim mugshots and court drawings stared back up at them. After the last two copied articles had landed on the floor, revealing their images of the younger Lankin at Rorschach and the fake Lankin in the background at the Carvel press conference, Nedly raised his eyebrows expectantly.

'So, what do we do now?'

'I was thinking maybe it's time to get a hot dog,' said Lil.

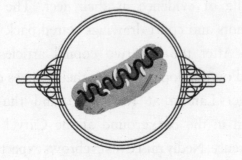

Chapter 14

How Do You Like Those Onions?

The corner of Fig Street was banked up with
piles of snow that looked like dirty fleece.

Lil and Nedly loitered a short distance away
from the hot dog cart, pretending to browse
the magazines at the newsstand on the other
side of the road.

Minnie the hot dog seller was wearing two
hats. Around her neck was a woollen snood, and
beneath the brown apron that was tied round
her waist she wore a padded jacket under a tatty

sheepskin body warmer. Her snow boots were too big but three thick layers of socks made up the difference. Even so, her freckled cheeks were dull and chapped-looking and the tip of her nose was so red it was almost glowing.

'She's not going to talk to you without Abe.'

Lil gave Nedly a ye-of-little-faith type look. 'Watch this.'

She slipped her way across the road but got held up climbing over the shovelled snow and by the time she had neared the cart a spry man in a black-leather bomber jacket and a Russian fur hat had beaten them to it.

Lil waited behind him, twiddling her pencil impatiently. Warm steam blew off Minnie's cart carrying with it the sweet smell of frying onions on the hotplate. Nedly drew up alongside and the man, who was still deciding on what to order, started shifting and looking warily over his shoulder. By the time Nedly realised what he had done, the man had scarpered, slipping over in the ice in his hurry to get away.

Nedly was mortified. Lil gave him a

sympathetic shrug that quickly morphed into to a look that meant, *On the bright side, we are at the front of the queue now*, and turned to the hot dog seller with what she hoped was a charming grin.

'What's up, Minnie?' With a wink Lil flicked her pencil onto the hot plate. Minnie expertly retrieved it with her tongs and offered it back to her.

'Sorry,' said Lil, reclaiming the greasy pencil. 'So –' she thinned her lips out and murmured stiffly through the side of them – 'What do you hear?'

Minnie narrowed her eyes at Lil. 'Me? Nothing.'

'It's all right, Minnie.' Lil dropped a second wink. 'We met a few months ago – I'm an associate of Abe Mandrel. The name's Potkin. Lil,' she added.

Recognition dawned on Minnie's face. 'Potkin? Say, maybe you do look familiar. 'So, what can I get you Potkin Lil?'

'It's the other way round,' Lil said, her ear tips going red.

Minnie looked confused. 'What can you get me?'

'No, I meant –'

'It's all right, kid. I was just ribbing you. Sure, I remember. You're Mandrel's sidekick.'

'Associate,' Lil corrected her, 'and what I'm looking for is information.'

Minnie shook her head. 'Is that right? Well, this here is a hot dog stand so . . .'

Lil realised her mistake immediately. She had forgotten she needed to buy a hot dog for cover. 'Oh, um, right. Sorry.' Her ears burnt painfully in the cold. 'I'll take one with the works,' she said loud enough for anyone who was listening to hear, winking again as she said the word 'works', and then, more quietly, 'and hold everything but the onion and ketchup.' She dug her hands into her pocket and pulled out a fistful of small change. There wasn't much to it.

'Actually, maybe I'll just take a bun. How much would that be?'

'Just one bun on its own is seventy.'

Nedly looked appraisingly at the hotplate. 'Maybe get some onions?'

Lil counted up the money in her palm. 'How much for the onions?'

Minnie sighed. 'That would be ninety all together.'

Lil beamed. 'Great – chuck a couple of those on too.'

'You want a bun with some onions in it?'

'Yeah, is that OK?' Minnie shrugged. 'And a thick slice of whatever else you've got.' Lil raised her eyebrows meaningfully and spoke out of the corner of her mouth again. 'By which I mean *information.*'

'You're a real piece of work, kid. All right – because you're a friend of Abe's I'll play ball. What is it you want to know?' She set to work on the bun – sawing it in half and flipping over some onions to get them good and brown, while Lil pretended to read the label of the bottle of mustard.

'What do you know about the Needle?'

Minnie frowned at the hotplate. 'The word

on the street is that the former prison governor Minos was being blackmailed and on the night he was killed, he had arranged to meet a reporter from the *Klaxon*, over at the multi-storey. He was ready to sing, only someone got to him first, and silenced him for good.'

'Anyone know who did it?'

'No one who's talking to me.'

'How about the epidemic?'

Minnie handed Lil the hot dog bun. It was soft and warm. 'The Secure Wing for the Criminally Insane is officially in lockdown. No one can get in; no one can get out. The epidemic was declared by the egghead in charge there, Dr Lankin. He used to work up at Rorschach.' She piled onions inside the bun. 'Not that anyone has reason to doubt him; by all accounts he's a stand-up guy.'

Lil and Nedly exchanged glances.

Lil squirted a careful line of ketchup across the onion bun and said, 'Rorschach burnt down years ago and Lankin only took up his post at the Needle after that other doctor, Carvel, got iced – I mean, burnt to death. So, anyone know where he was in between times?' She took a big bite that threatened to pull all of the onions out of the bun with it.

Minnie took a gulp of tea out of an 'I heart Peligan City' mug that must have been older than Lil was, and took a guess. 'Abroad?'

'Murmph.' Lil shrugged, chomping away, trying to disengage the onions.

Minnie looked thoughtful. 'Do you think he brought something back with him? Some kind of exotic germ?'

Lil shook her head vigorously. 'Mo,' she said, gulping away the half-chewed onions. 'I don't think he left town. I think he was here the whole time.' She levered up the Cryptic Eyebrow but Minnie didn't catch it.

'Whatever that epidemic is, it won't stay in there for ever,' Minnie murmured, drawing her body warmer closer, and looking uneasily in the direction of Nedly, who froze.

Very slowly he took a step to one side but the direction of Minnie's gaze didn't alter. She wasn't looking at him; she was looking into the distance where the Needle pierced the sky, its tip vanishing into snow clouds.

'I heard that quarantine has been breached,' she told them. 'Someone has another way in and they're using it.' Lil was poised to take another bite but decided against it, just in case. 'And Minos, and Ping, and all those big shots aside, I've heard that plenty of ordinary people have gone missing lately too, and then wound up dead and no one knows what they died from.'

Lil hesitated. 'You think it's connected?'

Minnie shrugged. 'Who knows?'

Lil wrapped a serviette round the remainder of her onion bun, stowing it away in her mac pocket for later. 'Have you heard if anyone is investigating? Like the police?'

Minnie smirked. 'Generally cops aren't interested in cases they can't solve, and no one cares about prisoners getting iced so long as whatever is in there doesn't get out.'

Lil gave Nedly a cynical look.

Minnie continued, 'But a couple of beat cops I know, Mucklehammer and Dingus, took an interest in following it up, trying to find out about some of the people round here who disappeared, but they were warned off by City Hall. They were told that there's a crack team working on the crimes and everyone else is locked out.'

'Is that true?'

'I wish I knew! Gordian isn't sloppy. She's got herself walled up in the Mayor's Office and no one between her and those shiny walls knows what's going on.'

'And the *Klaxon*?'

'They're on the case of the epidemic, so my guess is they have someone on the inside, just like they did with City Hall.'

'Randall Collar,' Lil breathed admiringly. 'So, do you think there will be someone like him in the prison? An undercover reporter?'

Minnie took a sip of the now cold tea, winced and chucked it on the snow. 'I'd bet on it.'

Lil chewed the end of the greasy pencil thoughtfully. 'Do you think anyone knows who it is?'

Minnie looked at Lil for a moment, like she was about to say something and then changed her mind. 'If they're any good, no one will know who they are.'

Lil spat a few crumbs of chewed wood out and gave Minnie the Penetrating Squint. 'Are you one of those people?'

Minnie turned back to her hotplate and rolled the dogs over with the tongs. Her fingers were red at the ends of her fingerless gloves and the nails were bitten close. 'Me?' She snorted a quick chuckle and flipped the onions a couple of times. 'I just sell hot dogs.'

Chapter 15

Scooped

The *Klaxon* wasn't delivered that morning, and neither was the flyer for the Black Pug Eatery.

Standing on the front-door mat Lil rubbed her eyes with the back of her hand and flicked through the pile of junk mail once again.

Nedly stared anxiously at the papers. 'Is it there?'

Lil gave him a tired look. 'No, it hasn't materialised since I last looked in this same pile a minute ago.' She unleashed a massive yawn.

'Sorry! I pulled an all-nighter to get my report typed up.' She tapped her rucksack happily. 'All ready for delivery.' The report was addressed to *PO Box 777, Peligan City*, where all submissions and tip-offs to the *Klaxon* newsdesk were sent. Although no such post office box really exisited; Lil had checked.

Nedly wasn't comforted. 'If this morning's edition hasn't come, maybe something is wrong at the *Klaxon* HQ? Maybe something has happened!' He gasped. 'Did you remember to put the index file boxes back in the reading room?'

Lil gritted her teeth. 'No, I forgot, but it can't be that. It's probably just been delivered to the wrong house.' They exchanged a look of dread. Suddenly feeling more awake Lil searched through the junk mail again, more thoroughly and with a hint of panic. 'Maybe there's been a bust?' Her eyes widened. 'Do you think we were followed there? I mean, I'm usually so careful, but I was really focused on getting the background on the spooks for my report – maybe I wasn't careful enough?

'We should get to the library, see if something is going down. Maybe we can get a lift.' She yelled up the stairs: 'Mum? Mum? MUM?' But Naomi wasn't there.

The bus into town didn't show up either. Lil and Nedly waited on the corner for thirty minutes and then started walking. The snow on the streets was so thick that it looked like a puffy reflection of the sky, the whiteness only broken up by the familiar grey of the buildings in between. Lil trudged doggedly onwards, dreading what they would find at the library but determined to see it anyway.

It wasn't until they reached the small row of shops a couple of blocks away that Lil realised they hadn't seen another person the whole morning. The compacted snow on the previously well-trodden paths was now mysteriously empty. She stopped and looked around. A face briefly appeared at a window only to be replaced by the swing of a curtain. Shop signs were unanimously turned to 'closed'.

And then suddenly there was a lot of people.

A crowd was gathered on the corner of Spooner Row, all looking dumbstruck and shaking their heads. Around them it looked like there had been a paper explosion: reams of newsprint bleeding grey ink were plastered onto windows and lamp posts; pages cartwheeled in the wind and became lodged in the snow.

Outside the newsagents a dispenser hung open, its glass-and-metal jaw dropping aghast, the lock jemmied off. Lil ran over to it and reached inside; a few papers remained, but it wasn't the advert-padded *Herald*. This paper was smaller and thinner, a folded news pamphlet. Lil knew before she laid her hands on it that it was the *Klaxon*. For the first time in their history, they had done a bumper print run – a big story, hot off the press. Too important to just reach their handful of subscribers, this was a story they thought everyone should know and they had gone all out to tell them.

The headline yelled a single bold word into the silence.

HAUNTED?

An exposé by Marsha Quake

For weeks a dark cloud has hung over Peligan City. This is not the rain cloud we're so familiar with. This is a cloud of menace and fear. Ordinary citizens have been kept in the dark while the city is held in the grip of a terrible foe. Within these pages we lay out the evidence highlighting the extent of the cover-up and an expert opinion from the man who helped us break the story, paranormal investigator Irving Starkey.

'What?' Lil looked up at Nedly, confused, her cheeks puffed out with incredulity.

Winter always hits Peligan City hard, but the Klaxon has been handed startling information that this time it's not the snow that's killing off our citizens, but something much more sinister.

Earlier this week the Herald boasted that homelessness in Peligan City was on the

decline. For once they were right: there are fewer people on the streets now than there were a month ago. But the reason for the downturn? Those people are now all dead. The winter death toll in Peligan City has more than octupled lately, according to sources in the Peligan City Police Department, but what is the cause?

The official explanation is exposure, but we have been given access to documents in a body of evidence known as the 'Fright File', which contains the post-mortem reports for at least twenty deaths over the last month. The victims in the file were all ascertained to have died not from exposure but from sudden heart failure, and in all cases the victims' hair had turned white and their expressions were frozen in terror.

One of the deaths has even been recorded on film. Leaked CCTV footage provides the most compelling evidence yet. The recording is from the multi-storey car park on the night of Governor Minos's murder earlier this week. The footage is low quality but it captures the moment when Minos's driver, Chris Manchurian, dies – you can't see what he is seeing but you can see the effect it has on him. His hair literally turns white as he opens his mouth to scream – and then he freezes. Within seconds Manchurian is stone dead.

The question on everyone's lips down at Klaxon HQ is: what did Manchurian see? What, or who, is stalking the streets of the city, frightening people to death?

Irving Starkey believes he knows. His theory is that Peligan City is under siege from dangerous spectres, ghosts that are invisible to the naked eye but are able to walk through walls, and terrify the life out of people.

There was an interview with Starkey on the next page, complete with a photograph of the man himself, looking into the middle distance in his hooded poncho, like a wacky revolutionary leader.

Does Starkey's theory hold any weight? Have the dead risen from the grave to plague the living? It's hard to swallow but the facts remain as follows:

There was a list of the recent deaths, their locations and headlines from the post-mortem reports, and what investigations, if any, had been carried out so far. It was a comprehensive piece with lots of convincing facts and figures that neither Lil nor Nedly read. They didn't need to.

Lil felt the pavement tilt slightly below her feet. It was the story she thought could never be printed, the one that no one would have believed, here in black and white.

Her fingers numbed with cold, she started reading the editorial comment:

If Starkey's theory is true, it may shed light on another mystery of our times: the increasing number of crimes perpetrated where no forensic evidence or witnesses of any kind have been found – crimes that for all intents

and purposes look like murder by an invisible killer. More on this in our next edition.

If the city really is being plagued by spectres two questions remain: what do they want, and how can we stop them?

There are no answers at City Hall. Acting Mayor Gordian has declined to comment.

Lil and Nedly stood shoulder to shoulder as they read. Neither one spoke but when they had finished they turned slowly, like mirror images, to face each other, their eyes wide.

Lil raised the *Klaxon* to face height and under the cover of the small newsprint screen she hissed to Nedly, 'They broke the story, the biggest one there's ever been. I had that story and I sat on it and now Quake has the scoop.'

Nedly peered round the paper and shivered. 'They know, all these people know the truth, about the ghosts. Look at their faces.'

Lil was too busy fuming. 'At least it explains what happened to the Fright File. Monbatsu was right: it was stolen.' She grimaced. 'I bet that's what Weasel handed Starkey at the Paranormal Society Meeting. The proof that his crackpot theory is true.'

She screwed up the article and kicked it at a bin. It missed and she had to go and retrieve it and drop it in properly. 'I can't believe I didn't have the guts to go for the scoop earlier. I knew more about this story than anyone. It was my chance and I blew it.' She kicked at a pile of snow, stubbing her toe on whatever hard metal object it had gathered around. 'Ow!' she whined painfully, and hung her head down, muttering, 'I just can't believe it!'

'I don't believe it either!' The sudden interruption of a passing woman in a thick knitted bobble hat and muffler made Lil jump. 'It's put the wind up everyone. I mean, ghosts!' She grinned incredulously. 'Whatever will they say next?' Then she looked down the road as if she felt something, a whisper on the back of her neck, the raising of goose pimples deep inside her wool coat, and the smile dropped from her face. She left them without a word.

Nedly looked after her in dismay. 'I gave that lady the creeps.'

'No you didn't,' Lil snorted. 'She gave them to herself. Come on, let's see what they're up to.'

A knot of people had gathered on the roadside. They were watching a shop window full of TVs broadcasting a live newsfeed from City Hall. Nedly shook his head. 'You go. I'm just making things worse.'

'Get over yourself – you're not that scary.' She gave him a reassuring smile. 'Come on!'

The crowd parted as Lil and Nedly drew near. People clutched their coats closer and looked fearfully at each other and then one by one they peeled away, leaving the two children standing alone.

Nedly frowned at Lil and she returned it with a helpless shrug. He was right – the atmosphere was thick with fear; a small scare caused a ripple, the ripple became a wave and soon the air around Peligan City was churning with it. A creak on the stair, a whisper of cold breath, and the ghostly presence of an unassuming eleven-year-old boy.

Acting Mayor Pam Gordian's muffled voice could just be heard behind the glass, telling people that an irresponsible and illegal news pamphlet had been spreading stories and had caused a civil panic. She advised the public not to be alarmed, and maintained that City Hall had everything in hand.

'Yeah right, they do!' Lil took out a pencil and started twiddling it agitatedly. 'I don't get it. These ghosts have been haunting Peligan City for weeks – why are people only acting like this now?'

'They probably thought it was all in their heads before, but here it is in black and white. They're being terrorised by invisible forces and no one knows how to stop them.'

Lil brightened. 'We do.' She tapped her pencil on the side of her nose with confidence. 'Come on, let's go to the library and have this out. This is all on Quake. She went to press without all the facts. We have to put them straight. If they knew one of the ghosts was on their side, then they wouldn't be so afraid.' She set off at a pace, crushing the snow underfoot.

Nedly called after her. 'I don't think this is the right time!'

Lil skidded to a halt as though a lightning bolt had struck her path, and whipped round. 'What? You're always saying that you want people to know about you.'

'I did, but now I think I'd rather no one knew what I am.'

'What you are?' She walked back towards him. 'Why are you talking like that? You're a ghost too, but so what? You're a good person, you're brave and you save people – Abe, me, you even tried to save Leonard Owl, and you beat Mr Grip. Most people would have run a mile but you didn't.'

Nedly looked away.

'The *Klaxon* only has half the story. Come on, it's up to us to put it right.'

'Can't we just go back home?

'You've got as much right to be in this city as anyone.'

Nedly bent over like he had a stomach ache. 'I just want to go home. I don't want to scare anyone else.'

Lil locked him eye to eye. 'Stop feeling sorry for yourself; we've got work to do. Now, I'm going to knock on a locked door, and I'm not going away until somebody opens it.'

Chapter 16

Exposé

Lil hammered on the door of the Librarian's Office. After a couple of minutes Logan flung it open, a furious look in her eye.

'I want to speak to Marsha Quake!' Lil demanded.

Logan pursed her lips and shrugged a 'Who?'

Lil narrowed her eyes into the Penetrating Squint. 'You know who.'

The librarian gave her a hard but considered

look and then began closing the door, but Lil stuck her foot in it. 'Not this time.'

Logan shook her head firmly.

'No way!' Lil shoved her shoulder between the door and the frame and tried unsuccessfully to lever it open with her body. 'You're not shutting me out,' she yelled into the office.

Her weight still braced against the door, Logan looked back over her shoulder at something Lil couldn't see. Then she sighed and took her hand off the door.

A voice called out from beyond. 'I'm afraid that Marsha Quake isn't here, Lil.'

'You know me?' Lil took a step forward, edging her way past the librarian. Nedly tried to pile in after her but got squished by the door as Logan stepped outside and closed it behind her. He melted through the wood with a 'Gah!' and immediately trod through Lil, who had stopped short. She gasped as the icy sensation struck her from behind and stumbled forward into the glare of a bright Anglepoise lamp that was aimed at her. Nedly darted into the corner.

He sat down quickly with his hands under his legs, and tried to keep out of the way.

The person who was seated behind the lamp was no more than a shadow. Lil could just make out the shape of their head and the curve of their ears. There was something about those lines that didn't add up.

'Who are you?'

'They call me Randall Collar, but that's just an alias. You know me by a different name.' The figure switched off the light. Lil blinked a few times, and then a few times more because she couldn't believe what she was looking at. Even as her lips started to form the word it lodged in her throat and she had trouble making it leave her mouth.

'Mum?'

'Hello, Lil.'

'You're Randall Collar?' Lil felt like she'd taken a kick to the guts. She staggered backwards until her heels hit the door and then she let it take her weight. 'It's you?'

'I'm sorry I couldn't tell you.'

'Because . . . ?'

'Because it was a secret.'

'And you didn't trust me to keep it?' Lil didn't need to try for the grim smile; it was on her face anyway. 'How long have you been hanging out here on my patch at the library?'

'The *Klaxon* has always been based here.'

'So Logan is in on it too?'

Naomi laughed warmly. 'Logan started it; the *Klaxon* was her idea. She's the editor. She showed me that profile article you did on that lady, Delilah. It showed a lot of promise.'

Lil's cheeks burnt with mixed feelings. 'Delilah is dead – did you know that?'

'No – I didn't.' Naomi got to her feet. 'I'm sorry.' Lil swerved her comforting hand.

They stood in silence for a moment, while Lil looked at an inky stain on the carpet, and then eventually she said: 'So you knew A. J. McNair?'

Naomi blew her cheeks out and switched on a small kettle in the corner of the office. 'That's another story. One thing at a time.'

'No!' Lil said firmly. 'Not one thing at a time. I want to know everything – right now.'

Naomi got two cups from the top of the filing cabinet and placed them by the kettle, which had started to make a low hissing sound, like an unspent breath being squeezed slowly from a corpse. 'A. J. McNair wasn't who you think he was.'

'Why doesn't that surprise me?'

'Here.' Naomi took a framed picture off the wall. 'This is the only picture we have of us all together.'

Lil stared at it. She saw her mother as a younger woman, just like in the photograph she had seen of her with Abe at the Nite Jar. She was wearing a beret, a turtleneck jumper and tortoiseshell glasses and sitting on a desk – the same desk she had been sitting behind when Lil came in. Next to her was a woman with long curly hair and a pencil skirt. Lil peered closer; standing behind them was Logan, in a checked blouse and slacks, smiling liberally with all her teeth. There were two men on either side of Logan, both wore white shirts with rolled-up sleeves, waistcoats and ties that hung loose.

'Which one is he?'

Naomi took the picture from her and gazed at it sadly. 'Lil, A. J. McNair isn't a person at all. It was a code name used by a group of undercover reporters so that we could speak the truth without fear of reprisals.' She turned the photograph towards Lil and pointed to each face in turn. 'Roland Selznick, me, Logan Mackay, Jessica Coltrane and Idris Canto.

'We had to create A. J. McNair, a mysterious fictional reporter who stood up against corruption in Peligan City, because as the truth became more dangerous we needed some kind of shield to hide behind. McNair was that shield. But he became much more than that, he became a symbol of resistance whose very existence gave Peligan hope.'

Lil's heart felt impossibly full. She couldn't believe what she was hearing. The water in the kettle started churning, bubbling up like voices

all talking at once. Her mother continued the story, her voice rising to counter the sound.

'An intrepid investigative reporter, never afraid to put his name to the truth, to bear witness to all the corruption and speak out against it. McNair was an example to everyone, and yet he was totally immune to intimidation, because he was so elusive – like a shadow.

'And then we were proved wrong.' The kettle clicked off and the room became suddenly very quiet. 'We thought he was invincible – but, of course, no one is.'

Naomi poured water over the teabags, watching them sink and then bob back to the surface. 'It was just before the election. Roland had dug up some pretty inflammatory evidence that Mayor Davious had been milking the public purse to finance his own property development company. At a press conference he popped some awkward questions, enough to get him thrown out. Davious went down a couple of points in the popularity rating after that, but Roland wasn't around to celebrate. When he didn't come in to work the next day we knew something was wrong.

'A few days later his body was dragged from the Kowpye River.' She stirred the tea slowly and then squeezed out the bags. 'Davious's retribution was crushing; that very day the *Chronicle* was closed down and in its stead the *Herald* was born. Its first headquarters were at City Hall.'

Naomi placed the mug of tea on the desk by Lil, sweeping aside the piles of documents and folders that were scattered there. Lil's eyes went automatically to the pile; all these stories, all the digging, it was everything she had ever wanted. Top-secret files, research notes, scribbles in the margins; a hive of industry bringing the real news to the real people. Her gaze lingered over one file in particular – a manila folder with a red-elastic fastening.

Naomi twisted the dial on the front of the filing cabinet back and forth and then opened it, rummaged for a few moments and pulled out an old newspaper, which she handed to Lil.

'Look.' It was the first ever issue of the *Herald*

and the cover story was the death of McNair. 'We didn't refute it. We didn't have any means to; Peligan City had seen the last of reporters openly speaking out against City Hall. The free press was gone, Roland had been killed and we let A. J. McNair die with him. We – and Peligan City – lost hope.'

Naomi looked at her daughter with shiny eyes. 'Roland was a great reporter. I wish you could have met him. You would have liked him. I did, I liked him a lot.'

Lil shrugged; she wasn't really listening any more. She had heard enough. Under the cover of the old *Herald* she slid the manila folder out from the pile. It was labelled 'Inquiry into Fellgate Prison'.

Her mother was still staring into the past. 'Roland died a hero but no one will ever know what he did.' She rubbed her eyes with her fingers, while silently Lil took hold of the folder and slipped it under her yellow mackintosh.

'As long as the only newspaper in circulation was the *Herald*, City Hall had the perfect tool to manipulate the citizens. We knew Roland's death should not have been in vain, there had to be another voice . . . and so Logan started the *Klaxon* and in Roland's memory we kept true to the spirit of McNair. Marsha Quake even wrote a fictionalised biography of McNair, *McNair and the Free Press*, something to inspire a new generation of journalists. Of course it was banned as soon as it was printed, but there are still copies in circulation. I used to have one.' She flicked her eyes up at Lil. 'Over the years the *Klaxon* endured, and once again the figure of McNair became a standard behind which the good people of Peligan City gathered. People like you, Lil, and people like me.

'For a long while I stood back and let the others carry on. You see, by then I had you, I had other things to worry about closer to home, like paying the rent and getting you through school. But as time went by I saw that things weren't getting any better, they only got worse, because things don't change unless people change them. The trouble was, so many people were just trying to get by; they didn't have any fight left in them by the end of the day.

'And then eight years ago I took a job at City Hall, working in the Public Records Department. An old colleague made contact one night and told me that they were working on a story, and they needed my help. I was perfectly positioned and as long as no one ever found out I could keep copying material for the *Klaxon*, helping them build their case to try to wipe out corruption at the top. Before long I was filing my own stories; to protect my identity I adopted the alias Randall Collar.

'I knew it was dangerous. I had more to lose than ever by then, but I had realised that not doing anything would mean a much greater loss – we stood to lose the city, our freedom . . . We stood to lose everything.'

Lil surreptitiously hoisted the folder higher under her mac so she could get a pincer hold on it through the fabric at the back of her pocket. 'It's a great story. Were you ever going to tell me?'

'I almost did, lots of times. A soon as Logan accepted that article I knew it wouldn't be long before you figured it out, and I wanted to be the one to tell you.'

Lil snorted through flared nostrils. 'You lied to me.'

'I never lied. I just –'

'Didn't tell the truth?'

Naomi gave a heavy sigh. 'I've had to make difficult decisions; I had to choose between the chance to save the city I loved, and you – my baby girl. And I chose you, Lil. You're more important to me than anything.'

'Is that right?' Lil's ears had turned a fiery shade of red, like two warning lights. 'You chose me?' She nearly choked on an unwanted tear. 'Look at where we are, look at what you're doing. You made a choice all right, that's pretty obvious – but you didn't choose me!'

Lil slammed the door so hard behind her that the sound reverberated through the room. Naomi stared at the space where her daughter had stood for a long time and then she let her body tip back until she was resting on the desk, gripping the edge tightly with both hands.

Nedly inched out of his corner. 'Don't worry,' he said softly. 'I'll go after her.'

Naomi sighed and wearily got to her feet. She walked right through Nedly on her way to the sideboard to sort the files that Lil had been playing with back into some kind of order.

Chapter 17

Haunted

The pavement under the viaduct was free from snow at least. Lil sat on the frozen ground, her prized copy of *McNair and the Free Press* was lying in the dirt at her feet and her ears were luminous and numb.

'Say something,' said Nedly, loitering anxiously in front of her.

Lil gave him an offhand snort. 'What's to say?'

'I don't know. I mean, are you OK?'

Lil shrugged it off, one-shouldered and half-hearted. 'Fine – I mean, my mum is the only family I have and it turns out I don't really know her at all, so . . .'

Nedly slunk down the brick wall to sit beside her. 'Sounds like she was in a pretty sticky situation. Remember how Craig Weasel came after us when he caught Abe sneaking around at City Hall that time? Imagine what he would have done to your mum if they'd found out she was the mole.'

'Obviously I wouldn't have told anyone. Not even Abe.' Lil pushed around an old crisp packet with the toe of her boot. Suddenly she looked up, eyes wide. 'Do you think Abe knew already?'

Nedly winced. 'Maybe. He did know your mum way back when she was on the *Chronicle* staff, and he was there in the Nite Jar that night, when that picture was taken, so he might have been in on the whole McNair thing. Maybe he knew the whole story.'

Lil let her head sink into her hands and rubbed

her eyes. 'He must have thought I was such a schmuck, playing the big reporter and not even realising that my own mother was the real deal.'

Nedly frowned disapprovingly at her. 'You don't really think that's what Abe would have thought.'

Lil let her shoulders sink with a sigh. 'Abe always said I was like Mum. I thought it was the ears.' She rubbed her eyes again; they were getting sore. 'What kind of investigator am I? I can't even see the truth when it's right in front of me.'

'You do have the same ears.' Nedly gave her a tentative grin.

This time Lil's snort was almost a laugh. 'I know.'

Behind the thick grey snow clouds the sun was sinking fast, already far below the high skyline of tower blocks. One by one the street lamps came on, glowing dimly at first.

Lil took a breath. 'It's just the idea that someone, Abe for instance –' she looked carefully at Nedly when she said this – 'knew a secret about my family that I didn't know. And they kept it from me.'

Nedly nodded quickly but his eyes went to the snow and stayed there. 'I suppose he didn't know how to tell you.'

Lil's grim smile resurfaced. 'Maybe. Anyway, it's done. No use in going over and over it.'

Nedly looked across at her. It was a look that carried a lot of meaning, enough to make Lil gulp and exchange the grim smile for the twitch of a real one. Then he said: 'How about that guy Roland?'

She was relieved at the change of subject. 'Yeah, that was pretty rough on him, getting rubbed out like that – especially as he wasn't even really McNair . . .'

Nedly tried again. 'No, but the way your mum talked about him, it sounded like he might have been –'

'He was just one of the gang. He was no more McNair than mum was. McNair was just a made-up person.' She swiped *McNair and the Free Press* off the ground, rolled it into a thick cylinder and squeezed it angrily. 'I can't believe I thought he was real; it's so obvious now. No one is that good. I've been such a sap. He wasn't a hero – he was a nobody. Literally.' She threw the book away and it skidded across the icy paving slabs and lay face down, stuck against the snow and soaking it up.

Overhead, a train thundered by. Lil reluctantly clambered to her feet. A fine snow was falling, drifting like mist and making halos round the street lamps. 'Come on,' she said, pulling up her hood.

Nedly watched her stomp away, and then looked over to where the book was lying forlornly in the snow. 'If you don't want that book any more, can I have it?'

'It's just a story. It's not real.'

'I know.'

'Fine.' Lil stormed back, picked up the book and put it in her bag.

They crossed at the corner, walked onto Arcade Street and stopped. A single corner shop was still lit up and open and, as they watched, a flurry of people spilled out of it, their arms laden with emergency rations of tins and toilet rolls.

The shop owner followed them out, turned the sign to 'closed' and then bolted the door in a hurry and pulled down the blind.

Nedly gave Lil a confused look. 'What's going on?'

Two lights appeared through the snow at the far end of the road and crawled towards them. The shoppers lined the roadside and stared as it passed. As the van drew near, Lil and Nedly saw a nervous driver at the wheel, shooting glances left to right as he ploughed onwards. Two horn speakers were strapped to the luggage rack. It was one of the Mayor's Office's electioneering wagons. A beaky, amplified voice boomed from the speakers, a recorded message playing on a loop.

'This is Acting Mayor Pam Gordian. Do not panic, City Hall has the situation under control. A curfew is in force; all citizens are instructed to stay inside after dark.' It was capped off with a burst of upbeat election music that echoed eerily in the hushed silence of the streets.

The snow was accumulating on Lil's shoulders as she and Nedly watched the van roll by, transfixed. 'It's the *Haunted* story,' Lil murmured. 'Now even City Hall is spooked.'

As soon as the van had turned the corner panic burst onto the scene as everyone tried to get off the streets as quickly as possible, which was hard in the thick and slippery snow.

A couple of stragglers hurried their way. They were padded out with layers of clothes, the collars of their jackets turned up and their woollen hats pulled down low. As they passed, the man stopped suddenly, his face turned ashen.

'There's something here!' he yelped, making Lil and Nedly jump. 'I felt it. A – a creepiness in the air – right there.' He pointed towards Lil, and Nedly started backing away. People across the road were watching, their eyes wide and filled with panic.

The woman tugged urgently on the man's sleeve. 'There's nothing there. Come on, you're scaring that little girl.' She put an arm through his and steered him along the pavement, but as she turned to go she cast a frightened glance over her shoulder and scanned the road for whatever it was that was making her heart pound.

'We'd better stay out of their way.' Lil nodded Nedly on to a side street, away from the people who were herding together, all trying to walk in the middle, no one wanting to be left behind.

Nedly looked miserably after them.

'Don't think for one minute that this is about you, because it's not,' Lil told him firmly. 'The ghosts they're scared of are the ones that have killed people, the ones who are frightening people to death. You couldn't scare someone to death if you tried.'

Nedly's mouth twisted into a small smile. It didn't reach his eyes at first – they stayed frozen, and then, a thaw. 'I did turn a patch of Abe's hair white.'

'Yeah, you scared him pretty well, but only to save his life. You would never harm anyone.'

'Aren't you scared? Of the other spooks, I mean?'

Lil shrugged. 'You went up against Mr Grip, and you did it to save me and Abe. And now I've seen a picture of that creep, I know how terrifying that must have been, but you beat him and he was the worst of the bunch. So, no, I'm not scared, not with you here.'

Nedly stuffed his hands in his pockets and kept his eyes on the pavement.

They waited at the bus stop again but when it became obvious there would be no bus coming they began the long walk home. It didn't matter. Lil was in no hurry to get back. As they passed beneath another railway bridge a train screamed by overhead, the brakes squealing as it cornered and then returned to the *click clack click clack* as it tore away, lit up like a phosphorescent eel, snaking its way through the deep sea of the early-evening sky.

Lil watched it go, wondering where it was heading and how much a ticket cost.

* * *

The street lights in Hen Road were on the blink. Yaroslava the toymaker stood on the pavement outside the old doll hospital, looking through the snow-dusted window. Every few minutes there was a buzzing, a clicking, a flickering of the lights and then the street was lost in fuzzy darkness and the snow a starlit dirty grey. A minute later they came on again, bleaching the snow and thickening the shadows, and so it went on. Yaroslava gulped back the jitters that were surging under all her layers of clothing and let her body sink down against the doorway until she was sitting in the porch, her head resting on the glass just below the 'closed' sign.

With a red-knuckled hand she cleared a window in the snowflakes that clung to the shop door and then wrapped her woollen undercoat closer.

The toymaker was able to pick out the familiar glint in the eyes of the toys lined up on the shelf, just as she had left them. Yaroslava's own eyes smiled back, but then hardened as her gaze reached the cabinet where those strange toys had been placed. There was something about them that frightened her, something about the expressions on their faces. Their cold, dead eyes. She had seen something like them once before, long ago, back in the old country, and the memory of it sent a shudder through her frozen bones.

Almost as if they too had picked up on the unease in the air, the street lamps hummed and blinked off and then on again. Yaroslava stared up at the nearest one, willing it to stay on. It did. She turned back to the workshop and saw straight away that something had changed. The door to the cabinet was open. She could clearly see the little figures in it staring lifelessly out into the room, and then she saw another. It was lying on the floor; it had fallen from its shelf and its blank face was tilted up slightly as if it was looking right at her.

Dread swept over Yaroslava. She cranked up her old knees and half ran, half fell into the road, her footsteps muffled by the snow, her hand searching her apron pocket for something she had placed there for safekeeping. Her breathing was ragged in the silent streets. As she reached the telephone box on the corner, the detective's card was already in her hand.

She shut herself in and picked up the receiver. Through the glass walls of the box the toymaker watched a flurry of snow change direction, leaving a dark gap in the blizzard. She peered at it, wiped the window and then looked again. The window of the phone box misted up suddenly as though someone had breathed on it from the other side and a doily of ice crystals formed on the glass.

Yaroslava's voice trembled as she whispered, 'Hello? Operator?'

'Which number do you require?' said the voice down the line.

The door to the box swung open. The toymaker stepped back away from it and looked out into the empty night beyond. She saw the street lamps go off one at a time as the darkness travelled towards her. Fear bolted her to the spot.

She grabbed the door of the box and pulled it shut again.

'Do you require some help?' the voice said. The lights in the box were the last to go out. 'Is this a prank call? You know the emergency services have got enough on their plates without timewasters like you clogging up the lines . . .'

It was then that she felt it. Whatever had been outside was now inside. There in the dark it was standing right beside her. With the last of the fight that was left in her the old woman threw her weight through the door, and with a cry that stopped her heart, she fell to the icy ground outside.

The receiver was left hanging down, twisting on the cord, the voice still talking although the booth was empty, and then the line went dead.

Chapter 18

The Secure Wing

Early the next morning on the outskirts of Peligan City South a stocky figure on bandy legs beetled his way across the snow, huffing and puffing along a narrow and slippery path down to the river.

Dressed in a hooded black raincoat and waders, Hench hurried beneath the mossy brick curve of the bridge and edged his way past the wreckage of buckled wheels and broken cookers that were lodged in the shallow waters and trapped by the softly frozen ice. Halfway under the bridge, he took a last furtive glance around him and vanished.

The entrance to the derelict storm drain was sealed off by heavy-duty barred gates, bound by a thick coil of chain. Hench dragged out the section holding the padlock from amongst a snaggle of water weeds, then he reached round his own neck and pulled out a key.

The darkness of the tunnel loomed. Hench tied his handkerchief round his face to block out the smell of sulphur and rot, and then splashed his way fearfully through the black oily water, to the dungeons below Fellgate Prison.

Cornelius Gallows was sitting at a table beneath the stark light of a single naked bulb, scrawling furiously in his notebook and eating a dinner of cold soup, which he had been spooning straight from the tin.

He looked up sharply as the dungeon door swung open.

'News?' His sunken eyes were cold and eager.

'Seen it, heard it! You can't move for the news.' Hench edged his way closer, past the hospital trolley and the machine. 'That newsletter that's always stirring up trouble, the one no one's supposed to read, they ran the story. The secret is out and everyone's terrified.'

'At last!' Gallows cried and the skin around his mouth wrinkled very slightly with mirth. 'The city is so very nearly in my grasp.'

He wrapped his long, pale fingers round the empty soup tin and squeezed it menacingly. The tin turned out to be deceptively strong. Gallows replaced it on the desk and picked up a discarded ball of paper instead and squeezed that until it was much smaller.

He laughed maniacally. 'My ghouls will bring Peligan City to its knees. It will look everywhere for salvation but only one person will be able to give it to them: he who controls the bogeymen!'

Hench's small eyes sparkled expectantly. 'Who will that be, boss?'

'Me, you colossal oaf!' They will have no option but to come to *me* for help!'

Gallows' laugh turned into a wheeze, which sobered him. 'Which reminds me, Gordian should be next, before she gets too comfortable in the Mayor's Office. I was thinking –' his eyes glimmered, the pale irises reflecting the bulb as a pinprick of light – 'that might be a job for Mr Grip.'

Hench stayed quiet. Gallows began drumming his fingernails on the desk, starting fast but then winding down to a tick-tock tempo that drew the seconds out. Finally his fingers were still. 'So, have you got them?'

Hench fumbled a drawstring bag out from under his raincoat, dropped it on the desk and stood waiting for instructions.

'Stop looming over me!' Gallows sniped at him. 'Stand over there in the corner.'

Reluctantly Hench shuffled backwards, but he didn't get too near the trolley.

'What's the matter with you?' Gallows scrutinised him. 'You're skittish.'

Hench let his sparkling blue eyes catch Gallows' cold, colourless ones for a moment and then he looked down. 'This stuff makes me nervous.'

Gallows looked at him with disgust. He reached into the bag and pulled out five figures from within and laid them side by side on the desk.

'I shall be requiring more, Hench, another five, at least. Bring them to me tomorrow night.'

'I—I don't know about that,' Hench stammered.

'Don't you?' Gallows leapt off his chair and scraped it across the cobbled floor with a grinding shriek. 'Sit down!'

Hench shuffled over to the seat and sat there, his hands on his trembling knees.

Gallows towered over him, shadows engulfing his sunken eyes. 'The way I see it, you have two choices, Hench. Do as I say and survive, or get in my way and perish. Hmm.' He looked up distractedly. 'That's almost a rhyme. If only

I could think of a terrible fate that rhymed with survive. Or a favourable outcome that rhymed with perish . . .'

Hench exhaled sharply. 'Things aren't going to plan, boss. It's Grip. He's been out again. He ran into someone –'

'Anyone of note?'

'No, but that isn't the thing. The thing is, that's twice now, and I didn't send him, so I reckon he must've woken himself up.' Hench blotted the oily sheen from his hairline. 'And the thing is, I had your assurance that these spooks couldn't wake themselves. You told me that they couldn't do anything without my say-so.'

'Hmmm,' Gallows said.

'So now I'm asking myself, am I safe? What if one of these spooks decides it would be fun to mess with me?'

Gallows looked critically at Hench. 'It is true that ever since Grip came back he's been a little difficult. If he wasn't so terrifyingly effective, perhaps I'd snuff him out for good.'

Hench muttered, 'You wouldn't like him so much if he was in here with you, giving you the creeps all the time.'

'Wouldn't I?' Gallows' eyes seemed to shrink back further into his skull. 'You underestimate me, Hench. I won't be in here for ever. All good things must come to an end and then I shall take over the task you are so obviously struggling with, of ministering extremely simple instructions. And, in the meantime, if you were to perish in an unfortunate accident I would just replace you with any number of other individuals I have at my disposal.' Gallows let his eyes drift upwards, past the dank brick ceiling and through the floors to the cells where the other prisoners were still sleeping. 'Mr Grip is, of course, the master of fear; he enjoys frightening people.' Gallows looked at Hench imperiously. 'He can sense your weakness, and so he exploits it. Conversely Mr Grip has nothing but respect for me. He was trapped in that decrepit old body, rotting away in that cell and now he's free. Well, in a manner of speaking.'

He brought his eyes back to bore into Hench's. 'I hold all the strings. The only person who is irreplaceable is me.'

Chapter 19

The Stolen File

Snow had fallen heavily overnight and wrapped the frozen city like a shroud.

At the soft knock at her door, Lil flopped quickly back under the covers, bundling the pillow over her head at the same time.

'Lil?' Her mother pushed the door open a crack and peered through. 'I thought you had work this morning. Do you need a lift in?' She stood there a moment, waiting. 'Or I could pick you up afterwards?' There was no reply from the bedclothes. She sat down next to the tense lump of duvet and rested her hand on it. 'Are you OK in there?'

There was a muffled, 'M'OK.'

'All right, well, I'll see you later.' Naomi left her hand on the duvet. If it hadn't been for the slight pressure Lil would have thought she was alone again, but the silence was heavy, and full of the stillness of two people holding their breath. Then the mattress sprang back and her mother left the room, quietly closing the door behind her.

As soon as Lil heard the Datsun splutter into life she jumped out of bed and ran down to the airing cupboard to fetch Nedly.

Fifteen minutes later they were ready to leave. Lil paused at the front door; for the first time since she had subscribed, she contemplated not taking the menu from the Black Pug Eatery off the mat, but old habits die hard. As she jammed it into her backpack, her hand brushed against something else she had stashed in there. Her fingers hovered by the folder and then ran along the red elastic that bound it shut. Maybe there would be a clue inside, definitely a story; it wouldn't have been at the *Klaxon* HQ otherwise.

Nedly peered over her shoulder.

'Ready?' he asked, his eyes searching for a sign that she was OK, back to the old Lil. It wasn't there, not yet.

Lil nodded. 'Ready.' She threw on her yellow raincoat and a scarf and then began the long cycle ride into work, with Nedly perched on the handlebars.

Lil pounded the pedals, her wheels spinning, throwing up slush as she sped down Angel Lane. Despite the freezing air buffeting her face she managed to force out snatches of conversation in between breaths.

'Let everyone else get spooked by the *Haunted* article; we've got a job to do. We have to stop these ghosts, just like you stopped Mr Grip; take them out, one by one. If we can separate them, it should be easier.'

Nedly didn't reply.

Lil continued, 'I mean, if we can break it down

into tasks, then it might seem more manageable. I'm not underestimating the problem.' She freewheeled round the corner, and then stood up to push along Shoe Lane, her mac streaming behind her like a yellow cape. 'We've still got to work out how to get into the prison, but I might have got my hands on something that will help with that.' She skidded to a halt at the traffic lights and then glared at the stop sign, squeezing the brake levers on and off while she waited.

'I'm not sure what the situation is with visiting the Secure Wing anyway, especially with the lockdown in place, but there must be another way in.' She hung a right and then started out on the final stretch, pedalling hard until she reached the road at the back of the Nite Jar.

As she coasted to a stop in front of the diner's backyard Nedly slipped lightly off the handlebars. 'But *you* could still get in; you could just pass through the walls, couldn't you?'

Nedly didn't reply. He walked a few paces along the pavement, leaving no trace in the freshly laid snow, then stood with his back to Lil.

She parked her bike up against the bins by the kitchen window, and called out to him. 'Are you coming?' Nedly didn't move. Lil retraced her steps, and dropped her voice to a whisper. 'I'd come with you if I could. I know it's a lot to ask. But you're the only one who can do it.' He didn't turn round. 'Nedly?'

When he finally spoke it was in a quiet voice: 'I never beat Grip.'

Lil huffed out a breath. 'Yeah, you did.' She thumped her gloved hands together a few times to warm them. 'At the battle of Yang Guang Heights, you said –'

'No, I didn't.' He turned to face her now. 'I just never denied it.'

Lil stopped clapping her hands and left them there, in mid-air, like she was carrying a small invisible box.

Nedly stepped towards her, his eyes dark and hollow. 'I thought I'd beaten him, but then, after he snatched me back, we both ended up, I don't know where, somewhere quiet. I just remember lots of streets, no lights, no noise. I

237

ran away and he came after me; I could hear his footsteps getting louder.' Nedly seemed to flicker slightly and Lil could see the pattern of the fence behind him emerging through his sweatshirt.

'It seemed like we had been running for ever, but then we heard this tiny bell ring out, and Grip stumbled. I carried on running, didn't look back until I had got to the other end of the street, but when I did I saw that Grip couldn't resist the sound; it was summoning him against his will, pulling him back, and he was snarling and scratching at the air.'

Lil, remembering the face from the newspaper story felt her skin crawl, and she shuddered.

Nedly continued, 'But he couldn't stop himself; the bell called him and he had to go. He skidded backwards like he was being pulled on an invisible string. He got further and further away until he was gone and I was alone.'

Nedly had faded so much now that Lil could only just hear his voice, only just see his lips moving. 'That was the last time I saw him.'

'So Mr Grip . . . ?'

'I think Gallows called him back. I think Mr Grip is still out there somewhere.'

Lil didn't look at him; she didn't want her eyes to betray her. She suddenly felt very cold and very sick.

'What do we do now?' Nedly whispered, staring at the toes of his trainers.

Lil's thoughts were whirling. If Nedly had beaten Mr Grip, who was without doubt the worst of the bunch, he could beat any of them. But he hadn't beaten Grip. Maybe he couldn't or maybe he was just too scared to try, but either way her plan, which was already shaky, was crumbling at the foundations.

'I'll think of something,' she said briskly. 'We're not done yet.'

As soon as Lil had stepped through the door of the Nite Jar Velma had said, 'We didn't think you'd come in today. With everything that's going on. You know you don't have to stay, if you'd feel safer at home?'

But Lil had shrugged. 'Is it all right if I stick around? I'd rather keep busy. You don't have to pay me or anything. It's just there's no one at home so . . .'

'Stay as long as you like.'

They didn't have any customers so Yoshi put on the radio and he and Velma sat at one of the booths and listened to old episodes of *The Edie and Oliver Show*, interspersed with the same public announcement broadcast: a counter statement from the acting mayor reassuring people that 'the clean-up of Peligan City would continue. On all fronts,' she had added ominously.

A City Hall employee came by and dropped off a bundle of leaflets – Velma pinned one up by the counter, next to the phone.

HAUNTING HOTLINE!
If you experience any of the following: a strong sensation of unease, sudden drop in temperature, unexplained noises and/or electrical disturbances, please call this number with your exact location immediately.

Underneath was a free phone number. The type was bold and in bright red ink and underneath in very small print it said:

Haunting Hotline is an initiative of Peligan City Hall. In the case of a genuine emergency there is no charge for this service.

Nedly frowned at it. 'What do you think would happen if you called the number?'

'Probably nothing.' Lil shrugged. 'I'd be surprised if anyone answered it. And even if they did, what could they do? Send in Irving Starkey?' She smirked at the idea.

By eleven o'clock the only things to wash up were their own breakfast plates and a few pots. Alone in the kitchen with Nedly, Lil sat on a high stool at the sink, absent-mindedly cleaning the egg off a pan by stirring the soapy water with a wooden spoon, while reading the morning edition of the *Klaxon*. Nedly perched nearby, on the counter beside the draining board.

There was a follow-up on the Fright File story, including a centre-page spread naming the confirmed victims. There were even photographs of the dead before they had fallen on hard times. Delilah's picture was a publicity shot taken from when she was a nightclub singer. She had a flower in her hair and glossy lipstick and she was smiling at something to the side of the photographer, or maybe she was just smiling to herself because she'd made it. She couldn't have known then what the future would hold.

Lil brooded on the picture. There were twenty other names on the list. Twenty people had died on the streets over the last couple of months. But only the high-profile deaths – Silverman, Ping and Minos – had made the papers.

There was also a map of the city with a cross for every location where the bodies had been found, and question marks for the bodies of the recent unusual deaths, including those assigned to the mysterious Firebug Killer.

'They've made the connection,' said Lil approvingly. She took out a pencil and joined the dots herself. 'If you just look at the crosses they're almost all over this side of town. Typical.'

Lil searched for Randall Collar's name but it only featured on a small update on the epidemic at the prison, berating Gordian for letting it go on unchecked and without proper medical support.

'They're not kidding,' she said. 'If they'd done something about it when the fake epidemic first broke out, then Gallows wouldn't have been able to form his deadly gang in the first place.' She laid the pamphlet on the drainer and gave the welded-on egg a really good scrub. 'Someone's got to stop that guy.'

'What guy?' Velma walked in and tipped the dregs out of two dirty cups, adding them to the bowl.

Lil's ears reddened. 'Yoshi, he burnt all the egg on the pan. See?' She held the pan in front of Velma's face and used the distraction to swipe the *Klaxon* from the drainer.

Velma smiled. 'I'll have a word with the management.'

Lil quickly washed up the cups and left them to dry. 'Can I have my break now?'

Velma looked at the three plates, two pots, coffee cups and slice that Lil had washed up in the two hours she had been there already and smiled. 'All right, but then you're mopping the floors. May as well get this place shipshape in case we ever get another customer.'

Lil picked up a waffle, hot off the grill, wrapped it in a paper serviette and took it out the back, under the corrugated iron lean-to where the industrial-sized bin was kept. She climbed up to sit on the lid and Nedly sat awkwardly beside her. Lil checked over her shoulder and then pulled the file out of her rucksack.

'Take a look at this. I happen to have come by some information on the prison.' She showed him the file.

Nedly moved closer. 'Where did you get it?'

'It was just lying around, in the *Klaxon* HQ.'

'You stole it?'

'I borrowed it.'

'Did you tell anyone you were borrowing it?'

Lil looked scandalised. 'I had just found out that everything I knew about my mother was a smoke screen, created to mask her true identity, and that she is really a hot-shot reporter working undercover for the *Klaxon*, the paper I've always wanted to write for, so . . . no.' She shrugged. 'I didn't ask. I thought maybe she owed me.'

She bent the file back to flatten it and then opened it between them. Inside were ten grainy blown-up photographs, all taken in low light and through bars. Lil flipped them over. On the back of each one was written 'Fellgate Prison, Secure Wing for the Criminally Insane' with the same date and number.

'Surveillance pictures,' whispered Lil reverentially. 'The *Klaxon* must have got someone on the inside.'

It was a sequence. Most of the pictures showed men in grey-striped prison uniforms, standing or sitting around in their cells, their faces and limbs blurred with movement. One showed a smudged profile of a tall man in a white coat with curly hair, a thick beard and spectacles. Cornelius Gallows in his 'Dr Lankin' disguise. In the next shot he was turned to look at something just out of frame and his mouth was open, as though he was speaking. Even pixelated in low resolution, his eyes appeared cold and empty of feeling.

The next picture showed another person beside him. This person wasn't wearing the prison outfit – he was dressed in a long, hooded black raincoat and he was offering Gallows what looked like a laundry bag.

In the final picture both men were looking directly at the camera – they must have spotted the photographer – and for the first time Lil could see the face behind the hood. It was heavy and potato-shaped with a dark shadow covering the jaw. She grabbed the photo so quickly that she practically screwed it up in her fist. 'Nedly, look here!'

She attempted to flatten it again, angled it at the weak daylight and fetched her magnifying glass out of her rucksack. 'Does he look familiar to you?'

Nedly leant in to study the picture more closely. 'It's the new owner of the doll hospital.'

They stared at each other for a moment, trying to work out what that meant. Lil took the first guess: 'So they're working together? Partners in crime?'

Nedly pointed to the laundry bag that the man was holding. 'What do you think is in there?'

Lil stared at it. 'Food, maybe? Or clothes?'

'So, he's taking Gallows supplies so he can hole up in the Needle for as long as it takes for him to execute all the prisoners and turn them into spooks?'

'That's how he's doing it. And then once he's done he can move on to his real target.' Lil pointed her finger out over the rooftops to the black-glass skyscraper; even through the snow City Hall glinted like a jet monolith. 'I bet he thinks if Gordian can't get this haunting under control, then only one person can.'

Nedly gulped. 'Me?'

'Gallows.' Lil's eyes softened. 'It's only a

matter of time before he makes his play for City Hall.'

'So, what can Gordian do?'

Lil shrugged. She pulled a pencil out of her back pocket and started chewing on the end of it. 'Gallows' spooks are too scary and there are too many for us to beat and I don't think either of us are clever enough to outwit an evil genius. There has to be another way.'

She looked down at the photograph, tapping it with her pencil. 'He's the weak link, Nedly. He's not locked away safely; he's here in the old town.' She pointed the lead tip at the new owner of the doll hospital and then her eyes grew wide. 'And what does he have plenty of that Gallows could use?'

'Aftershave?'

Lil puffed out her cheeks. 'Seriously?'

Nedly looked completely lost.

'Toys!' She gave him a triumphant grin. 'Remember what you said – when Mr Grip was chasing you, it was the bells that called him back. He must have some kind of object that he's bound to, just like Leonard Owl did. Gallows sewed those little bells on Wool so he could use him to control Owl's ghost, Mr Glimmer, and Owl was able to free himself by destroying Wool in the fire. Remember?'

Nedly nodded.

'If he's used the same technique with the ghosts from the Needle, then we won't need to defeat them, Nedly; we just have to destroy whatever object he has bound them to.' Lil pulled that morning's *Klaxon* out of her back pocket and opened it again at the map. She tapped a spot in the centre of the old town, where the most crosses orbited. The corner of Bead Street and Spooner row. 'What's here?'

'The picture house?'

Lil shook her head. 'On the other side of the road.' She turned the map round and Nedly cocked his head at it and then grimaced. 'The doll hospital.'

'I'll bet that's where Gallows is keeping them. Hidden amongst all the other toys.'

'Oh!' Nedly realised with a shudder.

Lil continued. 'You said the toymaker complained that there was something strange going on there at the doll hospital.' She bit her lip. 'If my theory is correct, she might be in danger.'

Nedly tried to follow her chain of thought. 'So you think that the spooks have been bound to toys and they're being kept at the doll hospital?'

'It's the perfect hiding place. No one would look twice.'

'But why wouldn't he just keep them close by at the prison?'

'Too risky. This "epidemic" can't go on for ever; sooner or later someone will get wise. The *Klaxon* are already investigating – these pictures are proof of that – and if his cover gets blown and he has to flee, he can't risk leaving the spooks behind – he'd never get them back.

'He will have thought through every eventuality; like when we turned up at the asylum, he had already claimed Lankin's identity and engineered his place at the prison so he could take over there as soon as Mr Glimmer killed Dr Carvel. If there's one thing we've come to know about Cornelius Gallows, it's that he's always one step ahead of the game.'

Nedly nodded knowingly. 'And he's really patient.'

'Yes.' Lil had to concede that one. 'They're the two things we've come to know.'

'And extremely cold and calculating,' Nedly added. Lil nodded, a little less enthusiastically. 'And he's a genius.'

When he opened his mouth to speak again Lil cut him off. 'I suppose when we really think about it we know quite a lot about Gallows.' She raised her eyebrow cryptically. 'And we're going to need every bit of that knowledge if we're going to put a stop to him. For good this time.'

She crumpled the paper serviette into her fist. 'So, as soon as the new owner leaves for the night, we're going to break into the doll hospital and find the haunted objects.'

Nedly slid down off the bin. 'What if he doesn't leave? Or what if he comes back?' He gave her an earnest look. 'We're going to need some help.'

Lil let the eyebrow collapse as she opened the bin and threw the balled-up serviette away with a sigh. 'I know.'

Chapter 20

The Bird Can Sing

Standing in front of the mirror Hench kept his eyes fixed on his own face and away from the dusty glass cabinet that was reflected over his shoulder. He knotted his yellow silk tie in a fat Windsor.

'You ain't going to spook me tonight, boys. I've got a couple of hours before I've got to make my delivery and I'm going to enjoy myself.' He looked at the drawstring bag, which was hanging on the wall filled with the next batch of poppets destined for the Needle. 'I'm going to get me down to the Golden Loop, maybe play a couple of spins on the wheel.' He gave himself a winner's smile. 'Why, you might ask? Because old Henchie deserves a bit of a break, that why. He's been working hard and not getting any praise for it, and the boss thinks staying here keeping watch on you freaks is no great shakes but it gets to you. Right here.' He jabbed a finger towards his temple and then tried to straighten his hat into a more upstanding position but it slipped on his oily hair and went back to its original perch.

Without his permission his reflection glanced nervously at the cabinet. The hair on the back of his neck rose with a prickle and he wiped a clammy palm to flatten it.

'Ha! The old heebie-jeebies! Nice try, boys, but Hench doesn't scare that easily. Am I right?' He asked his reflection.

His reflection wasn't sure.

His eyes darted again. The door to the cabinet looked like it was slightly ajar. Hench whipped

254

his head round to look at it. It was definitely open, but had it been before?

He cleared his throat and began a song; he knew how to beat the creeps. He'd beaten them before. '*Ta-dum, ta-dum, ta-doodah-dum.*' His voice was getting sticky. He loosened his tie a bit and dabbed the sweat off his face with his spotted handkerchief.

'*Dah-doo, dah-doo, tah-ah –*' The last word stuck in his throat as tight as a walnut in its shell.

Across the room a music box snapped open and the little crooked ballerina inside twirled lopsidedly to the same invented tune that he had just been singing. Hench moved over to it, his hand shaking. He pushed the lid closed. Behind him a clockwork monkey began to tick quietly.

Soft and silent, the door to the cabinet swung fully open and Hench watched, horror-struck, as one of the small figures inside fell forward and slipped from its shelf with a tinkling of bells.

He gasped, then pulled himself together. 'What did I tell you, Mr Grip?' He huffed his way to the poppet that was sprawled across the dirty floorboards and gingerly picked the limp body up.

'You got warned, Mr Grip. If I get any more trouble it will be the furnace for you, my boy. I don't care what the boss says.'

He hadn't mean to shake the poppet, but he had, and there it was: a sound like a shot from a pop gun, and then something knocked him out cold face down in the sawdust.

A second later his eyes opened cautiously, only this time it wasn't Hench looking through them. It was Mr Grip.

Hench's hand took a careful hold of the poppet on the floor and carried it to the workbench. His legs stumbled and jerked as though they were asleep; a couple of times they didn't plant right and he went down on his knees, bumping his head when his hands didn't shoot out to save him, but it didn't seem to bother him. When he reached the workbench he sat down, first on the floor with a jolt then he hauled himself up and sat on the stool.

Hench switched on the lamp, swiped all the tools onto the floor with a hand that collected splinters like a pin cushion collects pins, and then laid the poppet carefully on the bench. Smiling dopily at it, he gave it another gentle shake.

As the tiny bell rung Hench's ear pricked up. He opened his mouth a couple of times like a fish gulping for air and then whispered Grip's instructions to the poppet.

Hench's expression changed again: a broad smile broke out on his face and then vanished and like a puppet with cut strings he slumped forward onto the hard worktop fast enough to give himself a nose bleed.

The temperature in the room plummeted and the shadows lengthened. A spell of frost crept over the fur of the teddy bears as the malicious presence of Mr Grip left the body of Vassal Hench, seeped across the workshop and then exited through the front window without making a sound.

A few seconds later, when Hench woke up, he looked at the poppet and it stared right back up at him. Its black beaded eyes were blank. He felt a warm trickle on his upper lip, touched his fingers to it and found that there was blood; he upturned his palms and saw that they were speckled with splinters.

Hench's heart beat so loudly he could hear it, a deafening thump that filled his ears, a drumming that got louder until he snatched the poppet off the workbench by its bell and stomped off to a pile of crates that were stacked in the back room.

'No more mischief for you,' he whispered shakily.

He opened up one of the boxes and pulled out the red synthetic toy fur that was inside, laid the poppet at the very bottom, replaced the fur, then pressed the lid down hard. 'Let's see you get yourself out of there.' Then he stacked three more boxes on top of the crate and tapped the top one smugly.

Hench carefully closed the door of the cabinet that held the other poppets and then he put on

258

his thick astrakhan coat, switched off the lights and locked the front door behind him.

From a doorway across the street, Lil and Nedly watched as the lights went out in the old doll hospital. They saw the new owner disappear round the corner. The temperature had fallen with the night, soft and deadly, and the streets were eerily quiet. Moments later a shiny maroon Alvis pulled out of a side road, its lights sweeping the snow-covered road in a yellow arc. They waited until the glow of the back lights had disappeared and then they emerged from the shadows and set off for 154c Wilderness Lane.

When they arrived at the third-floor landing, they could hear a conversation coming from inside the office.

'He has a visitor,' Lil murmured. She inched her way towards the door, putting up a finger to warn Nedly to hang back, which he exchanged for a look that reminded her that he was invisible.

Lil drew nearer. It was her mother's voice.

'Her shift finished two hours ago.'

'Maybe she's gone to the pictures?'

'The cinema is shut; everything closes early with the curfew – everywhere but the library and the Nite Jar, and she's not at either one. Yoshi said she left at five.'

'Maybe you missed her.'

Lil pulled a face at Nedly and shuffled closer.

'Lil, wait!' he hissed.

'Shhh!' she replied. 'I can't hear.'

Her mother's voice dropped even lower. 'I know I'm putting you in an awkward position, Abe, maybe even asking you to break a promise, but I'm worried. She's my daughter and I need to know she's OK.'

'Why don't you ask her yourself?' Abe pulled open the door and Lil nearly fell through it. 'You know that's frosted glass, right?'

Lil managed to get the grim smile out just in time. 'I was about to knock.'

'Hey,' Naomi said, relief shining from her face. 'I was wondering where you were.'

'Sorry,' said Lil, not really sounding sorry.

Abe held the door open for enough time for anyone else who might have been on the landing to walk through it and then closed it again with a shiver.

Lil dumped her rucksack on the desk. 'I've got to talk to Abe about a case we're working on.' She paused. 'It's private.'

'I can keep a secret.'

Lil hardened her heart. 'We don't want the press involved at this point. If there's a story in it, we'll let you know.'

Naomi held her hands up in surrender. 'OK, leave me out of it. That's fine. I'm just glad you're all right.' She waited but Lil stayed silent, so eventually she backed over towards the sofa. 'I'll just wait in the corner. You won't even know I'm here.'

Lil rolled her eyes. She unzipped the rucksack and pulled out the copies she had made of the newspaper articles about the executed prisoners, laying them all out on the desk for Abe to look over.

Lil sat watching him as he took it all in. He was a careful reader and she could see his eyes scanning back and forth, like a shuttle on a loom as he tried to weave this new information into what he knew already. Every now and then he rubbed his chin. When he'd finished he muttered grimly, 'So this is who we're up against. It adds up with Montbatsu's theory, though I wish it didn't. What I can't see is how is he getting to them?' He dropped his voice to a mumble. 'Gallows, I mean. How does he know when they're going to croak?'

'Read on.' Lil passed him the stolen file.

Naomi piped up from the arm of the sofa. 'I wondered where that had gone.'

'I just borrowed it,' said Lil, manoeuvring to block her mother's view.

'See anyone you know?' Lil asked Abe, her eyes gleaming.

Abe analysed the photo. 'That –' he stuck his finger against the pudgy face in the hooded raincoat – 'is Vassal Hench. I put him away fifteen years ago for armed robbery.'

'Oh. Right.' Lil nodded. 'But actually I wasn't talking about him and anyway, he's out now. What's more, he's the new owner of the doll hospital out on Hen Road.'

'Is that right?' Abe growled, glaring at the picture, daring it to agree with him.

Naomi called over. 'He's the one that's been breaching security. That picture was taken only three days ago.'

Lil gave her mother a warning glance and then turned back to Abe. 'He's working with Cornelius Gallows; he can get in and out of the Secure Wing whenever he wants.'

Abe looked sceptical. 'Why would he risk it – doesn't he know about the epidemic?'

Lil flashed her eyes at him. 'There isn't one. Gallows is executing the prisoners.'

Abe slapped his forehead with his rubber palm, catching himself in the eye with one of the bendy fingers.

Naomi edged out from the corner. 'Are you talking about Cornelius Gallows? Ramon LeTeef's old partner in crime?'

'The very same.'

'Didn't Gallows die in the fire at Rorschach?'

Lil gave an exasperated sigh. 'Look, this is a complicated story and we don't really have time to explain.'

Abe was winking fitfully as he tried to focus on the photo while wiping away tears. 'But how is Gallows getting into the prison – the same way as Hench?'

'He's already there. He has been for months. Look.' She tried again, pointing to Gallows.

Abe held the picture up under the Anglepoise lamp, closed his injured eye and glared with his good one. 'Is that Lankin?'

'No!' Lil and Nedly cried out at the same time. Lil rummaged around in her rucksack until she found the older article and put it under Abe's nose. 'This is Alector Lankin, taken thirteen years ago, at Rorschach Asylum.' She put the

264

surveillance picture beside it. 'And this is him now. Notice anything different?'

Lil, Abe and Nedly all crowded around the desk lamp to stare at the photograph, while Naomi hovered behind.

Abe pondered it. 'He hasn't aged well.' Nedly leant over his shoulder, causing goose pimples to spike on Abe's neck as the creeps set in. 'Do you mind giving me a bit of space here?' he growled.

'Sorry.' Naomi backed away. 'I wasn't trying to pry.'

'I didn't mean –' Abe started but then didn't know how to finish. He turned back to the photograph. 'He looks thinner.'

'Yes,' agreed Lil, casting Nedly a vexed look. 'But also, if you look closely, you'll see that he's managed to grow half a foot taller, and his face is completely different.'

Abe placed a rubber fingertip over the older Lankin's curly hair. 'Hey!' he exclaimed suddenly. 'Cornelius Gallows, as I live and breathe! So that's where he's been hiding, pretending to be Lankin, all this time.' He looked up at Lil, his jaw set in steel, the fires of justice burning in his eyes. 'I'll tell you something, I bet the real Dr Lankin never even escaped the original fire at the asylum.' Lil looked patiently back at him and the light in his eyes guttered. 'You guessed that already?'

'I – we – had a hunch,' she confessed.

'That's pretty good investigative work,' Abe admitted. 'Chip off the old block, eh?' He smiled up at Naomi but she was busy studying the map that was pinned to his wall and if she heard the comment, she didn't let on.

'So,' Lil continued, ignoring him, 'like you said, Monbatsu was right, the cases are connected, Gallows has been executing prisoners and then sending his gang –' she dropped her voice to a whisper – 'by which I mean "ghosts", after the kingpins of Peligan City, like Minos and Ping, and Silverman, and the ones in the Fright File are those who got in their way.'

She nodded him further out of earshot and continued. 'But we've got a good idea about where he's keeping the things that his spooks are bound to and we're going there to destroy them. Abe, we're up against a deadline of the deadliest kind . . .' She was about to say, *and we need your help* when she remembered her mother was there, so instead she said, 'And we thought you might want to come along, but it looks like you're busy so . . .'

'Everyone is busy tonight,' Naomi said firmly. 'And we need to get home. If it snows again, we might not get past the ring road. You don't have to tell me what's going on if it's a big secret, but whatever it is, it can wait.' She gave Abe a pointed look.

'Lil, I'd like you and the file you borrowed from me in the car in five minutes, OK? Say your goodbyes – I'll be waiting.'

She made for the door with Nedly trooping behind. 'Wait!' Lil shouted after him. Naomi turned. Lil shuffled the photos together, and handed them over, flashing a look to Nedly that meant 'stay put!' 'You might as well take this now. I've done with it.'

Naomi nodded. It was a look of sad

acceptance, and it stayed with her as she walked away. Lil waited until Naomi was clear and then turned to Abe. 'So, are you coming?'

'Just you try and go without me.' He grinned and Lil grinned back at him. 'But we're not going to make the mistake we made last time,' he continued. 'This time we wait until it's light, and then we go in. I'm not doing any more poking around in the dark in haunted houses.'

Lil had stopped grinning. 'But Hench will be back tomorrow!'

'Let me handle Hench.'

'But what about the toymaker? She might be in danger! We need to warn her.'

'She's my client; if there's any warning to do, I'll do it.' Abe's nostrils flared a couple of times with the deep breaths that blew out of them. 'What do you think your mother would say if she knew we were going off to an old doll hospital to fight ghouls all night?'

'Obviously I wasn't going to tell her.'

'Well, she's waiting for you outside so I'd say you're all out of options tonight.' Abe gave her a look that held a sigh in it. 'I'll come by in the Zodiac first thing tomorrow and we'll go after Hench together. I promise.'

When Lil got to the bottom of the stairs she paused for no more than a millisecond and then took a sharp right, turning away from the front door and following the hairpin bend of the hallway towards the back of the building.

Nedly jogged along in her wake. 'Why are we going this way?'

Lil found what she was looking for: the back door. 'Because Mum's out there waiting, and I'm not ready to go home just yet.'

She slid the bolts across, squeezing the handle until it turned, and opened the door to the street behind. A shaft of cool lamplight stretched along the hall. Lil's shadow sliced it in two and fell on Nedly. The road beyond was dotted with drains over which the snow had melted, like black spots on white dice.

Lil stepped out from the doorway and the door began closing.

Nedly hesitated. 'We're not going to the doll hospital on our own, are we?' He saw Lil turn back towards him through the narrowing window of the doorway and started forward. He almost made the gap, but by then it was only a few centimetres wide, and with a shuddering 'Yaargh!' he spilled out onto the street and ran after Lil who was already halfway down the road.

Up in the office Abe rubbed his palm over his jaw. It made a rasping sound like someone sandpapering a pumice stone. He walked the floor a couple of times and then paused at the map of Peligan City. His eyes traced the pattern of streets until they reached Hen Road. Burying both hands in his pockets he nodded to himself, and then looked down at Margaret. She looked back at him from under her steepled brows.

'All right, you can have your walk,' he said, ruffling her head fur. 'Let me get my hat.'

The phone rang as they got to the door, so urgently that it seemed to rattle with every bell.

Abe sighed and turned back. He picked up the receiver. 'Hello?'

The voice on the other end was deep and measured. 'That you, Mandrel?'

'Monbatsu?'

'You should get down here. Another body has just come in. Same cause of death as the others: white hair, terrified expression.'

'I appreciate the tip but I've got to be somewhere right now.' Abe looked at his watch.

'She was holding your business card when they found her.'

Abe let the receiver drop for a second as his face drained of colour. 'Have you got a name yet?'

'Stanislav, Yaroslava,' Monbatsu told him. 'They called her the toymaker.'

Abe whispered a 'thanks' and hung up the phone, chewing his lip, and then he stuffed his torch into his mac pocket and with a look of grim determination he made his way down the stairs and out onto Wilderness Lane, with Margaret hot on his heels. He exchanged his prosthetic hand for his driving attachment and tipped down the brim of his hat against the freezing night air.

The Zodiac was covered with snow and the door was frozen shut, but after a few minutes of grunting and pulling at it he managed to get it open. When he turned the key the engine just gave a chesty groan and died. He tried thumping the steering wheel and growling at it, but its last breath had been final.

Margaret lay down on the front seat with her head between her paws and Abe closed his eyes and clenched his jaw. He was about to get out and walk when his lids burnt orange, and when he opened them he found himself dazzled by the glare of the yellow headlights that had appeared in his rear-view mirror.

Chapter 21

Hide-and-seek

Nedly's face appeared as a pale smudge, looking out through the dirty glass window of the doll hospital. He glanced up at Lil for just long enough to mouth *Almost there!* and then went back to glaring and pointing his glowing finger at the window latch.

Lil tried to look patient and encouraging but she was standing atop the curved metal lid of an aluminium bin in the alley outside and the frost had made it slippery so she didn't dare move her feet.

'There!' The latch flew up.

Lil had her penknife ready. She traced the window opening a couple of times, cutting through the paint.

'Don't be too long.' Nedly poked his head through the glass. 'I don't like it in here on my own.'

'I'm being as quick as I can.' Lil stuck the blade through and levered it a few times until, finally, the long-closed window popped open. She pocketed the knife and pulled herself up quickly in case the frame gave way.

Crouched on the window recess she took her torch out of her mac pocket and shined it below.

'How did you get up here?' she whispered.

'I climbed on those boxes.'

Lil gave the tower of cardboard a cautious poke; it swayed slightly. She didn't fancy her chances, so with a sigh she repocketed the torch and lowered herself as far as she could until she was hanging by her fingers, and then dropped, further than she would have liked, to the floor. 'If we have to make a quick getaway, I might have to exit through the door.'

'Or stack up some more sturdy boxes? There are tonnes here,' Nedly said, and there were.

Lil let her torch beam follow the toy-covered shelves that lined every inch of the room, right down to the ground where they were partially covered by crates and boxes. She had a creepy feeling they were being watched but that could have been the hundreds of toys lined up on the shelves who all seemed to be looking in their direction. The underlying smell of sawdust, turpentine and paint was comforting; the lingering scent of Hench's potent aftershave lotion was not.

'What do you think?' she asked Nedly. 'Are you picking anything up? I'm nervous, but I think that's just because we've broken into the lair of a known associate of an evil genius.'

'Hmmm,' he agreed. 'There's definitely a weird atmosphere in here but I haven't seen any spooks.'

'So maybe they're sleeping.'

Nedly turned to her with an ominous look in his eyes. 'Or hiding.'

Lil tried to hold the torch beam steady as she surveyed the rest of the workshop. The torch had been the first thing she'd bought with her wages from the Nite Jar, and so far she hadn't had much chance to use it. She had always imagined that when they finally uncovered Gallows' trail Abe would be there too and they would seek him out together. It hadn't crossed her mind that she and Nedly would have to go it alone.

She let the beam trace the shelves opposite. Every type of doll was lined up there in battalions. They looked abandoned, maybe forgotten.

Pale-faced china dolls with soft bodies and sticky hair, teddies, tin soldiers and plastic action figures, waxy-looking toys with bendy rubber limbs and clockwork mechanicals . . . a particular shiver crept over her skin when she saw the moth-eaten knitted animals.

'It's going to take hours to check all of these.'

To their right was a huge and heavy workbench with an Anglepoise lamp crooked over it. The surface was covered in a chaos of fur, tiny scattered nails that looked like iron filings and metal implements of the kind you might find in an unlicensed operating theatre. A row of vices were clamped onto one side and there was a little wooden stool that was fastened to the bench by a sturdy hinge and polished to a high shine by the seat of someone's trousers.

Behind it were free-standing shelves filled with everything you would need to fix things. Coils of wire, bobbins, dried-up pots of glue with gummy, balding brushes stuck in them, unlabelled bottles of solvents in various colours, oil cans and tiny rusted tins of paint with battered lids.

Past the workbench and shelves was a doorway without a door that led to a small back room. Lil began walking towards it when she saw something move out of the corner of her eye, a pale flash; she back-tracked quietly, stifling a gasp as a distorted version of her own face appeared in the dirty glass door of a wall cabinet right in front of her. Lil pulled her jumper over her sleeve to wipe it and then lifted her torch to look through the darkened glass.

'Lil!' Nedly called to her.

'What?' she hissed, following him. In the back room was the toymaker's bed: an old armchair with a knitted blanket draped across it, a pot-bellied stove and a little white sink with a grimy curtain that hung down from the bowl. A portable TV sat on top of a big wooden bookcase that was stuffed with paperback novels. Lil accidently kicked over a mug that had been left on the floor with a thin layer of fossilised tea at the bottom of it. It rolled over to where Nedly was standing, passed through him and bounced off the skirting board on the other side.

'There's another floor,' he said. 'A basement.' He nodded towards an open door that led to a stairwell.

As Lil made her way down the concrete steps, following the spot of her torch as it was swallowed up in the gloom, the hair on the back of her neck was prickling. From deep inside the basement there was a low roaring sound. At the end of a short corridor a door was ajar and Lil could see a light flickering softly behind it, like a candle.

She nodded to Nedly to go first. He shook his head. *Go on* – she nodded more vigorously. *No way!* he mouthed back. Lil rolled her eyes. Mouthing '*fine*' and then '*whatever*', she pushed up her sleeves, took a deep breath and then continued on alone. The dancing orange light on the basement wall made her draw back for a second, as she cautiously pushed the door open, but it was just the firelight from the window of a large cylinder-shaped furnace, with wide copper pipes that sprung from it like legs and plunged into the floor and ceiling. That was where all the noise was coming from.

Nedly peered over Lil's shoulder. 'You know what this means?'

She pointed upwards. 'That must be where Delilah's old pitch is.'

'I didn't think of that,' Nedly admitted. 'Yes, but also it means we have a way to destroy the toys – when we find them we can burn them up right here.'

'Good plan.' Lil grinned at him, her face lit by the orange flames. 'Come on, we better get to work.'

They backed out of the furnace room. Lil was about to put her foot on the first step of the stairwell when they heard the sound of the shop bell ringing

Chapter 22

Deal or No Deal

Alone in his office, in the Secure Wing for the Criminally Insane, Cornelius Gallows was challenging himself to a fifth game of Scrabble.

Oblivious to the din from the frightened inmates, who were running their tin bowls along the bars of their cells, trying in vain to get someone's attention, he picked up the letter 'X' and turned it thoughtfully in his long, delicate fingers, pondering his next move. He had beaten himself in every game he had played that evening, in every game he had ever played. He always won in the end.

From somewhere in the wing he heard a door slam but ignored it. The life that went on outside his office didn't interest him. The men in the cells were no more than fuel for his ghost-generating machine. He had no fear of them – they relied on him for food, heating, water – without him they would have none of it. He was the only one that mattered to the outside world. The Brave Dr Lankin.

Gallows afforded himself a thin-lipped laugh, which caught somewhere in his bony chest and rattled it.

The cells had fallen silent. Gallows wound his scarf closer round his neck. It was certainly chillier than normal, although cold lurked permanently in the stones of the prison. He glanced at the thermometer on the wall behind him: it was four degrees. Significantly colder than normal. Now it was three degrees, two . . . one. The mercury dropped further and the air around him began to freeze.

'Who is there?' he snapped, and his breath curled out in a fog.

In response the Scrabble board leapt off the desk, flipping the tiles upwards like tiny pancakes, where they hung in mid-air, floating before his eyes.

Gallows let one hairless brow arch slightly.

'Impressive. Who sent you?'

Four of the letters dropped onto the board and began coalescing into words.

I DID.

Gallows' deep-set eyes narrowed. 'Clever boy. I presume I'm talking to Mr Grip.'

There was a pause, and then more letters rained down. They slid around the board until they spelled the word GRAINNE.

Gallows snatched tiles out of the air and placed them against the word to spell out:

GRAINNE IS DEAD.

The word DEAD was swiped instantly from the board. They hit the wall and dropped to the floor and in their place came the word HERE.

The vein in Gallows' forehead began to visibly pulse. 'Very well. I imagine you've gone to some lengths for an audience with me, your maker. What is it that you want?'

TROUBLE. The word appeared on the board and then dispersed and another was formed, BOY.

'Trouble with a boy! Why don't you just kill him?'

ALREADY DEAD

'One of your victims?'

There was another pause and then a flurry of activity as letters swam together.

ONE OF YOURS

Gallows rolled his eyes. 'You, the most vicious and feared serial killer Peligan City has ever known, afraid of a boy?

Mr Grip stayed silent for a moment while a feeling of menace spread through the room, making even Gallows give a small shudder.

STRONGER

'How can the ghost of a boy possibly be stronger than that of a grown man?'

HE IS FREE

Gallows gave a theatrical sigh and and ran his hand lightly over his fine spray of hair.

'So that's what you want.' There was a pause. 'What possible benefit would that be to me?'

I WILL DESTROY HIM

Gallows considered the letter tiles irritably for a moment. 'If I were to free you, how could I be sure you will come back?'

The letters were still, and then they moved.

PARTNERS

Gallows inadvertently let out a snort of disbelief, which caused the temperature to drop another two degrees; nevertheless nostalgia began to cloud his eyes. 'I had a partner in crime once.' And then they hardened again. 'It didn't end well for me. But then he never took me seriously, not until it was too late.' Gallows rubbed his smooth chin thoughtfully. 'Genius that I am, I don't even know if I can free you.'

TRY

Gallows' face turned very pale pink, and a blue vein twitched at his temple. 'If you lose your binding, I'll have no way to call you back. If you pass over, that's it.'

The letters remained still but the crushing feeling of dread was making the air thick. Gallows' breaths were becoming shallow and his narrow shoulders shook slightly.

'Fine,' he agreed begrudgingly. 'But as soon as you've beaten the boy I want you back here.

'I must admit that with your exceptional ghoulish powers it would be handy to have you as my new goon. And it's true that of late Hench has let his fear get the better of him, plus he has no real sense of loyalty, whereas you . . . I made you who you are today. With my calculating genius and your bloodcurdling psychopathy we would make quite the pair.' Gallows' fingers fluttered excitedly, and then they were still. 'But you must agree – you will be second in command. I am the boss. Swear it. Swear you won't betray me.'

I SWEAR

'Let me think a moment.'

As Gallows closed his eyes and turned his

brilliant mind to calculating just how he could reverse his experimental procedure and sever the connection that Mr Grip had with the material world without destroying his ghost completely, it occurred to him that it wouldn't matter too much if the operation did end badly for Mr Grip. After all, he could be so very disobedient. No, on reflection Gallows couldn't lose. He made a mental note of the equation needed and then opened his eyes and with a lifeless smile he said, 'Eureka.'

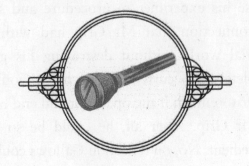

Chapter 23

Nothing But Creepy Toys

A dark figure stood in the doorway of the doll hospital, backlit by the street lamp outside. Lil and Nedly swapped anxious glances and then they heard the click of a switch and the room was awash with the unforgiving glare of the strip light.

It was Abe.

'So you came?' Lil bent down to scratch Margaret's ears and hide the smile that betrayed her relief. Abe stepped awkwardly to one side to reveal Naomi standing behind him and Lil's smile vanished.

'You! You followed me?'

'No,' Naomi replied honestly.

'She followed me,' Abe confessed.

'Great, some detective you are.'

Abe took that one on the chin. He gave her a sombre look. 'I just took a call from Monbatsu at the Morgue – the toymaker is dead.'

'We're too late,' Nedly whispered.

Lil laid her hand on Margaret's tufty head. The little dog met her gaze with sorrowful eyes.

Naomi bobbed down beside them. Her glasses had fogged up in the warm workshop. She peeled off a glove and wiped her finger over the lenses. 'You're supposed to be at home.'

Lil dipped her eyes and muttered. 'So are you.'

They crouched in silence while Naomi tugged off the other glove finger by finger and then she tilted her head down low, until she was in Lil's sightline. 'I figured I'd come by and find out what was so important that you had to give me the slip.'

Lil got to her feet. 'You wouldn't understand.' She walked over to where Nedly stood and opened a random drawer that turned out to be full of patched-up dolls' clothes and pretended to sort through them.

'Try me.'

Nedly raised his eyebrows hopefully, but Lil murmured, 'She doesn't know anything about this. She'll just get in the way.'

'Give her a chance,' said Nedly.

Lil blew out her cheeks and turned to face her mother. 'We're looking for some toys.'

'Looks like you came to the right place.' A smile crinkled Naomi's eyes.

'This is serious. They're very dangerous toys –'

The crinkle straightened. 'How are they "dangerous"?'

'They've been tampered with and now we have to destroy them.' She steeled herself. 'It has something to do with the ghosts that are terrorising the city.'

Naomi started to speak but Lil interrupted her. 'I know. I know you don't believe in it.

But if you're going to stay here and help you're going to have to trust me. We're not here for the scoop; we've got work to do.'

Abe moved away from the doorway. He trod heavily as he crossed the room as if he were weighing every step, until he was standing beside Lil. He took a deep breath and squared his shoulders. 'It is true, Naomi. Lil knows her onions. I'll vouch for that. Quake's story, the haunting of Peligan City. We knew all about it, before it broke, I mean. We've known for a while and –' He cleared his throat. 'I don't have time to explain right now – but we do have a pretty tight theory that the person controlling the ghosts is doing it by means of some objects that we think he's keeping here.'

Lil gulped in the silence that followed. Her eyes slid sideways to Abe, who was trying to hold his chin up at a dignified angle while maintaining Naomi's troubled gaze.

'So,' he continued, 'we aim to destroy them before he catches on, wakes them up and sends them after us.' He nodded gravely at her. 'I know how it sounds, but that's the tall and short of it.'

'O-K,' Naomi said uncertainly, with a look of someone who's wondering whether she's dreaming or everyone else is. 'Don't take this the wrong way, either of you, but how is it that you know so much about it?'

Lil couldn't stop herself executing an almost-perfect Cryptic Eyebrow raise at her mum. 'We've seen this sort of thing before.'

'Have you?' Naomi turned to Abe and narrowed her eyes. 'Really?'

Abe tried to laugh it off in a strange combination of snorts, shrugs and the occasional 'ha!', then he leant on the end of one of the shelves, which pitched under his weight and jettisoned a row of soft-bodied clowns into the air.

He grabbed a couple of fistfuls and stuffed them hurriedly back onto the shelf where they slumped forward like they had bellyache.

'Yes,' said Lil matter-of-factly. 'You see, I have secrets too.'

She and Naomi stood in silence for a few seconds, neither one looking away.

'If we're all going to work together,' said Nedly. 'We're going to need some kind of a plan.'

Lil nodded imperceptibly. 'OK, Mum, Abe. Listen up.'

She pushed all the pots, bobbins and tools off the top of the workbench with the sleeve of her mac and threw down a couple of handfuls of sawdust, scattering it thinly. Then she picked up an old cane someone had used for stirring paint.

Abe, Naomi and Nedly gathered round. Along the shelves, rows and rows of glassy-eyed dolls watched in silence.

'All right. Once we have found the right toys we're going to need to destroy them as soon as possible. We can't afford to waste time if one gets set off accidentally while we're searching.' She glanced over at Nedly and he gave her a reassuring thumbs-up. 'Here's the workshop,' Lil said, drawing a large rectangle in the dust with the cane pointer. Then she drew a circle. 'And that's me.'

She put in a dividing line of shelving across the rectangle to create the back room. 'It'll be faster if we do it in a kind of throwing relay. Mum, you wait here at the top of the stairs.' She added a couple of lines for the stairwell and sketched another circle. 'I'll throw each toy we find to you, then as fast as you can you throw it downstairs for Margaret, here.' Lil tapped the bench. Margaret was too small to see the plan in the dust, but she cocked her ears at the mention of her name.

'What about me?' said Abe.

'Tell them about the furnace,' Nedly cut in eagerly.

'Give me a minute, will you?' Lil muttered at him.

'Sorry, I –' Abe buried his chin in his crumpled collar.

Lil sighed. She had run out of bench. 'It's not to scale,' she explained as she squished in a thin sausage-shaped room right at the edge.

'Abe, you'll be down here.' She tapped the sausage with the pointer and made a tiny circle. 'Right by the furnace. That's how we're going to destroy them.'

'Where do I fit in?' Nedly asked.

Lil let the cane rest on the sawdust in the corner of the workshop. It left a small dot behind, a fifth circle in the dust. Abe saw it too and nodded.

'Keep an eye out,' Lil murmured to Nedly and then she raised her voice again. 'But first we have to find these haunted toys.'

Abe pulled off his rubber hand and flexed his pliers. Naomi pushed up the sleeves of her camel-hair coat and scanned the shelves. 'This place has nothing but creepy toys. What are we looking for?' She scrutinised the faces of a row of baby dolls in front of her, pausing at one with a lazy eye whose hair looked like it had been cut by a buzz saw. 'How about this one?' She reached up to grab it.

'Stop!' cried Nedly, Abe and Lil all at the same time.

'You didn't warn her about the bells,' Nedly added.

'There's one thing we forgot to mention.' Lil gingerly picked up the doll to examine it. Very lightly she gave it a shake. Breathing out she replaced it. 'The ones we're looking for will have bells on them or inside them to make a noise. We're going to have to shake them to see if they're the right ones but very carefully, because as soon as we do the spooks will start coming. That's why we have to act fast.' She took a deep breath. 'Ready? OK, let's do it!'

Dust floated in the air as they set to work.

'Hey, Lil!' Nedly piped up. He was standing on a cardboard box and searching along the high shelves. Lil stood on a crate to join him and came face to face with a balding clockwork monkey in a threadbare silk waistcoat. It was brandishing cymbals and the sort of smile you would have if you were being electrocuted.

She winced at it and murmured, 'This one is horrible.'

Very carefully she shook it. Nothing happened.

Lil started to return it to the shelf and then paused. With trembling fingers she turned the cold metal key in the monkey's back. The ticking of a mechanism unwinding filled the silence but the arms stayed still. It was broken.

Abe was working his way down a line of teddy bears, his hand finally coming to rest on a saggy-chested bear with a shiny bald pate and misty eyes.

He smiled at its kindly face, and then the smile vanished and he murmured: 'Please, not you.' He gave the bear a gentle shake. The straw in its body rustled. Abe breathed a sigh of relief, stretched up to replace it and then thought twice and stuffed it into the pocket of his mac. He looked up furtively to find Naomi staring at him, eyebrows raised.

'Ha! Caught me red-handed!' He held up his pliers in surrender. 'There's a kid that Lil knows down at the orphanage, his toy got destroyed a while ago and I figured this might be a good replacement.' He squashed the bear further into his pocket.

Naomi smiled then took a step sideways and bumped against a wooden crate. She peered inside; it was full of pale sack-cloth poppets, mannekin-shaped with a topknot of cloth on their heads where the material had been gathered and tied. Some were featureless but others had black-thread crosses for eyes, a single stitch for a mouth.

'These ones are horrible!' she said. 'And there must be more than fifty here. Tell me these aren't the ones we're looking for?'

Abe looked over at the crate and poked a couple of the poppets with the end of his pliers.

'I can't see any bells attached, but maybe there's something inside that could make a noise?'

Naomi swiped the nearest poppet and shook it, while the others held their breath. There was no sound, so they all exhaled and Naomi chucked it back into the pile.

As Abe straightened up he came face to face with his dusty reflection in the cabinet. He wiped his hand across the glass and saw a shelf full of the same sack-cloth poppets.

Each one had a tiny silver bell tied round its topknot.

Naomi peered over his shoulder. 'Like those ones?'

Abe croaked, 'Yeah, that would do it.'

They all stood looking at the poppets who stared disconcertingly back with their crosses for eyes. Their cloth bodies had mouldered and sagged, pulling their mouths downwards.

'OK,' said Lil, breaking the silence. 'Let's get to work.'

Abe, Naomi and Margaret left to take up their positions while Nedly stood by the window in the opposite corner to Lil, where he had the best vantage point to watch for the other ghosts.

Very slowly, Lil extracted the first poppet, holding it by its little bell to stifle the ringing. She ordered her hand to stop shaking but it just got worse. The grey body jiggered beneath her fingers, its damp cloth face brushed her palm and she nearly let go.

She blinked. *Why was she hesitating? It was*

just a doll. But somewhere sleeping behind those cross-eyes was a murderer, and in a second it would wake. Doubts crept in and stretched their spiky limbs; this was her idea, and if she'd got it wrong then one of them could die. Maybe Abe. Maybe her mother.

'I'm ready, Lil! Give it your best shot!' Naomi yelled from the back room.

Lil looked at Nedly, and he nodded encouragingly back at her: *Do it!*

She swallowed hard and took a deep breath, pulled her arm back and swung it low. 'Incoming!' she shouted, as soon as the poppet had left her hand. Lil watched it turn somersaults in the air, arms and legs wheeling. She heard the little bell on its head tinkling softly as it soared above the other toys, and then over the dividing shelves and out of her sight.

'Whoops!' Naomi exclaimed. 'Dropped it.'

The temperature began to plummet

'Here they come,' said Nedly.

'Throw it to Margaret now!' Lil shouted. Her breath curled out, a white wisp on the freezing

301

air and the plastic toys on the shelf all turned to look at her. There was a beat of silence and then she heard the tiny bell ring out once more as Naomi hurled the poppet.

The strip light flickered. Nedly's wide eyes tracked sideways as something crossed the room, towards the basement, following the sound.

At the bottom of the stairwell Margaret leapt, curling her body to propel herself upwards, and snatched the poppet out of the air with a toothy grimace. She hit the floor at a run, high-tailing away from the thing on the stairs, down the short corridor to the furnace room where she skidded to a halt, her claws skating over the concrete floor. She released the poppet at the same time as Abe's multi-use pliers reached for it and in one fluid movement he hurled it into the flames.

The light stabilised and the temperature rose again.

Lil peered round the shelves into the back room. 'Are you OK, Mum?'

Naomi shrugged brightly back at her and said, 'I don't think that was too bad.'

Lil's skin was dewy with cold sweat. She shook her head. 'We have to be faster than that.'

In the minutes that followed the frenzied relay played out, the room dropping to freezing as ghost after ghost woke up bewildered, only to be extinguished again when their poppet was incinerated, until they only had one to go.

The last remaining poppet on the shelf glared coolly at Lil, who shivered and gave it the Squint. Outside in the street a car door slammed; at the sound the poppet flopped suddenly forward and slid from the shelf. 'No!' Lil cried, swiping it off the floor and pulling back her arm to hurl it.

'Lil! Hide!' Nedly shouted.

She ducked, fumbling the shot. The sound of the small bells ringing was drowned out by the ding of the shop bell as the front door opened. Lil threw herself behind the workbench and squatted there, heart pounding. She let her head drop back against the side of the bench and counted to three, trying to slow her breathing down, trying not to gasp back too much of the sawdusty air and then, as quietly as she could, she peered round the corner.

The new owner was back.

Chapter 24

Invisible Friends

The man they now knew to be Vassal Hench was standing motionless in the middle of the room, with only his too-blue eyes moving, taking in the scene: the ransacked shelves, the cabinet door open, all the poppets gone. Lil heard the creak of the floorboards as he crossed the workshop towards her.

'Nedly,' she whispered.

'Stay down!' he yelled at her. 'He's coming your way.'

She tried to squeeze herself into the space under the workbench, tried to make herself as narrow as possible. She screwed her eyes shut as if that would make her smaller and then opened one eye a crack so she could still see what was happening.

The shadow came first, followed by the man. Lil saw a pointed brown shoe and a chequered trouser leg pass her by and go straight through into the back room, creaking all the way. Nedly followed after a couple of beats. Then the creaking stopped.

'Oh no –' Nedly began.

Lil scrambled to her knees and looked past the sticky glue pots, through the dividing shelves and into the back room where her mother was.

Naomi spotted the poppet on the floor before she noticed Hench. She bent down to pick it up, just as he put the pointed toe of his patent-leather winkle-pickers on it.

'Not so fast,' he said.

Naomi tried to yank it out from under his

shoe but only succeed in tearing its arm off. She stepped back, out of his reach.

Hench smirked. 'Aren't you a little old to be playing with toys?' He stooped down, picked up the poppet very carefully, and pointed it at Naomi.

'Hands up, baby,' he snarled. 'Nice and steady.'

Naomi didn't put her hands up. At that moment she was the only person at the doll hospital who wasn't afraid of a doll. 'Who are you?' she said.

'I'm the owner of this establishment, so the real question is, who are *you*?'

'I was just passing and I saw the light on.' Naomi tried to look neighbourly. 'Thought maybe something was up.'

Hench wasn't buying it. 'You here on your own?'

Naomi hesitated for a second and then yelled, 'Abe? Can you come up here for a minute. Please?' She gave Hench an amiable smile. Her eyes didn't flicker away from his, not for a second. 'I came here with a friend – he's just down there. Checking to see if anything is up. Like I said.'

They all listened to Abe's weary tread on the stairs. 'Is that all of them?' he asked as he emerged from the basement, sweating from the furnace and with his trilby tipped backwards. When he saw Hench with the poppet in his hand and Naomi's warning glance he slowed, coming to a halt at her side.

Hench eyed him suspiciously. 'Have we met before?'

'I'm sure I'd remember you,' Abe growled back at him, tugging down the brim of his hat.

Naomi dropped the severed arm at her feet. 'We should probably go now.'

Hench shook his head. 'I think you should stay.'

'Really, we have an appointment in town.'

'I'm sure no one will mind if you're late.' Hench grinned at her.

'Look –' Naomi began.

Hench stretched out the arm that held the poppet and pointed it at her. 'Really, I insist.'

Abe stared at the poppet. 'All right, pal, you're holding all the cards; we'll come quietly.' He held up his hands.

Hench nodded at Abe's Swiss-army attachment. 'Put down the pliers.'

'I can't.'

Hench pointed the poppet cautiously in his direction. 'Don't mess with me.'

'Sincerely. It's a fixture.' Very slowly he pulled his sleeve down to show Hench the leather-clad socket. 'See?'

'Still looks pretty useful to me. Hand it over. Nice and easy.'

Lil watched from behind the glue pots as Abe unstrapped his Swiss Army hand and placed it reluctantly on the floor. 'Be careful with it.'

Hench laughed and kicked it out of Abe's reach.

'Now, where are the others?'

Naomi gave him a hard stare. 'What others?'

'Don't act stupid with me – the other ones like Mr Inch here.' As he lifted up the poppet in his hand, the bell gave a tiny tinkle and he sucked in a breath. 'Now look what you've made me do.' He stared daggers at Naomi.

They all stood in silence; the air seemed to buzz, like a cloud of flies was moving in from far away. A bead of sweat trickled down from Hench's temple.

After a long moment he exhaled. 'All right. You got lucky there. Let's go.'

Lil watched Hench back her mother and Abe towards the stairwell. As they neared it Naomi glanced quickly in the direction of the shelves. Hench clocked it. 'Anyone else here I should know about?'

Naomi shook her head.

Abe said, 'I've got a dog.'

'Congratulations.'

'I mean down there – in the basement.'

'Well, you'll need all the company you can get. You might be staying some time.' Hench disappeared from Lil's view as he shepherded Abe and Naomi downstairs, leaving his shadow to trail behind him. 'And if I forget all about you, you can always eat it, am I right?'

From down below they could hear Margaret growling, like the sound of a very small car revving up and about to burn some serious rubber.

Lil crept into the back room, picked up Abe's Swiss Army hand and stuffed it in her rucksack. Then she took out her pencil, chewing it furiously while her mind raced through potential action plans.

Nedly paced around. 'Now what are we going to do?'

'I'm thinking as quickly as I can.' Lil kept her voice low. 'We're on our own but we have a chance. First, can you kill the lights?'

Nedly glared at the strip light. The electricity inside it began to sizzle, the bulbs grew dazzling for a moment and then with a series of *ping*s they went out one by one.

Lil nodded. The full moon left a grey shine on everything, but it would do. 'He's scared of that poppet he's holding, maybe almost as much as we are. Lucky for us he hasn't woken the ghost up yet.'

Nedly gulped. 'She was already awake.'

'What!' Lil choked on a bit of chewed wood and had to suppress a cough. Her eyes watered with the effort.

Nedly gulped again and lowered his voice. 'Mr Inch isn't a "mister" at all. It's Grima Cadiz, the Grey Hood. That woman who used to work in the courthouse, remember?' He didn't need to say any more. Lil remembered.

'She's wearing the . . .' He indicated pulling something down over his head. Lil broke into a sweat; her chest seemed to have contracted so there was no way of getting enough air into it. 'She woke up when you threw the poppet.'

'So, where is she now?'

Nedly nodded at the doorway to the basement. 'Waiting for instructions.'

'OK,' Lil whispered, just loud enough so that she could hear her own voice over her heartbeat and the rush of blood in her ears. 'Here's the plan. Hench doesn't know about you, so you're our secret weapon. He won't be able to tell you and Inch apart.'

Nedly cast a nervous glance at the basement doorway. 'You want me to put the frighteners on him?'

'As soon as his guard is down I'll go for the poppet.'

'Sounds risky.'

Lil felt around below the workbench; she found a gap between two dustbins and squished herself into it, tucking her mac round her. Nedly crouched in front of the shelves behind. 'He's got Mum and Abe trapped down there and there's still one poppet in the game. Nedly, it's up to us . . . We're their only hope.'

They heard footsteps on the stairs. Lil held her breath.

Hench walked slowly across the workshop. The moon reversed the lettering on the window and laid it out in shadow across the floorboards. When he reached the front door he flicked the light switch a few times and then rubbed a palm over his clammy jaw.

Lil tried to stay calm; she took a deep breath and then gave Nedly a small but confident smile and a nod that meant. 'OK – do it.'

Nedly stepped up to Hench. At once the temperature started to fall. Even in the fuzzy darkness, Lil could see a web of ice form on the surface of some old spilled paint on the floor in front of her.

Hench tried to stifle a shiver; he held Inch's poppet by the head, squashing it inside his fist to keep the bell from ringing and letting its legs dangle. Walking slowly along the shelves in the workshop, he used the tip of his stubby finger to nudge boxes and reams of fabric aside, mumbling, 'Poisoner, swindler, mugger . . . Where have they put you all?'

He opened a tall wooden cabinet and appraised the contents, which were mostly doll parts. One of the heads rolled suddenly off the shelf and bounced on the floor. Hench put out a foot to steady it and the doll's eye dropped down in a slow wink. Instinctively he toe-punted it away.

'Mr Inch. Is that you?' he whispered, casting a frightened glance at a nearby tower of crates.

The air in the workshop had started to freeze

and Hench's shallow breaths appeared in tiny puffs in front of him. 'At ease, Mr Inch,' he hissed. 'You stay where you are.'

Hench took a gold engraved lighter from his pocket and struck it. The lazy yellow flame swayed, stretching shadows in the warm glow it created.

Nedly blew it out.

'Stop fooling around,' Hench yelled at the poppet in his hand. 'I tell you what to do; just sit quietly in the corner – wait for instructions.' He bashed the poppet on the side of his palm, muttering to himself, 'Why aren't you working properly? Why aren't you doing what you are told?'

There was a sound like the flutter of wings, and Hench whipped round, his eyes wide with panic as a hard plastic fairy doll swooped down from the top shelf and struck him with a miniature karate chop on the nose. He held the poppet right up to his face and snarled: 'Don't mess with me, Inch!' The sounds of the TV sparking into action came from the next room.

'You have to do what I say! Those are the rules!' He shook the poppet over and over again. Its little bell ring-dinging madly in protest.

Nedly rushed at a shelving unit and a whole row of jars flew into the air and smashed onto the floor, spilling their contents all over the place. Hench ran in to see what had happened and slipped on the glass eyes that had scattered. He went over hard on his back and the poppet slipped from his grasp. Lil darted forward and made a grab for it but Hench was faster; he snatched it out of her reach and scrambled to his feet.

'Not so fast . . . Hey, ain't you the little girl who was looking for her dolly?' He peered at her in the low light.

'That's right.' Lil's eyes went to the poppet in Hench's grasp.

'Oh no', he chuckled. 'This one ain't for you.' He darted forward and made a grab for Lil. She shrieked, ducked out of the way and threw her pencil at him.

'Yaargh!' It caught Hench in the face and he staggered back, clutching his fist to his eye socket.

Lil fled into the back room, looked hopelessly for somewhere to hide, and then dropped to her knees and scrambled beneath the sink, pulling the curtains round her until there was just a thin crack where the two sides met.

Hench's lumbering body blocked the moonlight that was streaming through the window as he passed the shelves that divided the room. 'That wasn't very nice,' he said, knuckling his eye socket. Floorboards creaked as he lumbered forward.

Lil's trembling knees were pushing against the curtains, the toes of her boots peeking out from under it. She realised with a surge of panic that she wasn't really hidden at all, and cut her losses. 'Nedly!' she cried out. 'Do something!'

The crack in the curtain darkened suddenly.

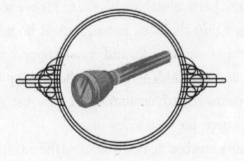

Chapter 25

The Last Poppet

Hench swivelled just in time to see what was coming but not fast enough to escape it.

The floorboards groaned as they took the weight of the toppling bookcase. The TV skidded from its perch, and struck Hench on the top of his head, skimming like a boulder over his oily hair and dive-bombing the floor where it sprang apart with a crunch as it hit. A wave of paperbacks quickly followed and pelted Hench from all angles. He crooked his elbows over his head as finally the bookcase fell, hitting him with a blow that floored him instantly, knocking the poppet out of his hands and burying him amidst the pages of the *Classic Westerns Collection*.

Down in the basement everyone stared at the ceiling.

'What was that?' Naomi gasped. 'It sounded close. You don't think Lil . . . ?'

The glow from the furnace deepened the shadows in Abe's furrowed brow. 'Lil will have gone to get help; she's a smart kid.'

Margaret peered up at him from under the tufts of her eyebrows and rested her head on her paws.

Abe started pacing. He glared at the locked door, and worked his jaw like he was chewing on an iron spring. 'If that goon hadn't taken my Swiss Army hand, I could have gotten us out of here by now.'

Naomi cupped her ear to the metal grille of a ventilation shaft cut into the wall. She closed her eyes and listened hard. 'What if she didn't go? What if she's still up there alone?'

'She won't be –' Abe looked like he wanted to say something else; he opened his mouth a few times, and then gave up and closed it.

Naomi stared past the grille into the square black tunnel beyond. 'We can't just sit around here waiting. If there's any chance she's still up there, she needs help.' She rummaged around in her pockets, took a coin out and used the edge of it to turn the old screws that held the grille in place. 'This could be a way out.' Once two of the screws were on the floor Naomi took hold of the edge of the grille and yanked it away from the wall.

Abe peered doubtfully into the hole. 'That's way too small for you to get through.' He took the discarded grille from her and held it up against himself. 'Let alone me.'

Naomi wiped the sweat off her forehead and left a rusty smear there instead. 'I wasn't thinking of either of us.' She looked at Abe and then they both looked down.

Margaret stared back at them.

Lil poked Hench's hand gingerly with the toe of her boot. It lay bent and motionless, like a dead spider.

'He's out cold.'

Nedly looked sickened. 'Do you think I've killed him?'

Lil knelt down and reluctantly held her fingers to Hench's wrist to feel for a pulse. It was there – a surprisingly strong one. 'No, it's OK. He's alive.' Nedly sagged with relief.

The poppet lay on the floor a few inches away from Hench's hand.

'Where's Inch now?'

'She's sitting in the corner just like Hench asked her to.'

Lil tried to slide her glance from under her eyelids to the empty armchair in the corner. At least it looked empty.

Nedly dropped his voice even further so he was almost mouthing the words as he said, 'We need to get her poppet sorted as soon as possible. I think once she realises what we're planning she will try and stop us.'

Lil nodded. 'OK. And we'll need to get the Key to the furnace room off Hench, so we can get Mum and Abe out and the poppet in.'

She bent down carefully, and stretched her hand towards the poppet. Her fingers grazed the sack-cloth body. She shuffled nearer, reached again and Hench's hand suddenly sprang to life, grabbing her ankle. Lil screamed. He pulled her over and she went down with a gasp, cracking her knees, and smacking her hands on the hard floor just as Hench burst out from under the pile of books, Godzilla-like with a roar, pushing the bookcase aside and staggering to his feet.

A frantic thumping noise struck up from the cellar. Lil opened her mouth to shout for help but her breath was snatched away as Hench lashed out again, grabbing her by the hood of her mac. Lil jabbed him as hard as she could in his pod-like belly, but he just scrunched the collar tighter round her neck. Nedly was looking around for something heavy to throw at him when suddenly a flash of sandy-coloured fur flew out of the ventilation shaft, sending the rusted grille clattering to the floor.

Margaret tore across the room and sprang at Hench, clamping her small but sharp teeth round his wrist like a pearl-toothed vice.

'Yoweraghhh!' Hench cried, letting go of Lil. He grabbed Margaret by the scruff of the neck with his other hand. She yelped as he tried to wrench her away.

With a flash of luminescence Nedly rushed at Hench, his jaw set, his eyes black and furious. Hench tumbled backwards, releasing Margaret who scampered away with her fur on end.

As the dust settled around them, Hench lay back on the pile of toys, grey-faced, his bitten wrist buried in his armpit.

From the basement Lil could hear Naomi frantically yelling, 'LIL!' through the ventilation shaft.

'Mum? I'm OK!' Lil shouted back. She peered down the shaft and then kneeled down beside

Margaret and spoke in a soft voice. 'It's all right, girl. It's all right.' She reached out a hand and gently stroked Margaret's spiky scruff. 'You were very brave coming to find us, but now you need to go back.'

Margaret tilted her head to one side with a worried look. 'We'll be OK.' She gave her forehead a reassuring rub and then looked over to Nedly. He glanced fleetingly at the 'empty chair' and nodded. 'I want you to find Abe.' Margaret cocked her ears. 'And I want you to take this.' Lil stretched her hand out and carefully picked up Inch's poppet. She held it out to Margaret who looked apprehensively at it and then at the chair in the corner, her neck hair spiked again and her forehead wrinkled. 'Please,' Lil added, and Margaret took it gingerly between her teeth.

'And as quickly as possible.' She picked the little dog up and pushed her into the mouth of the ventilation shaft shouting, 'Now! Go, go, go!'

The telltale bells tinkled urgently as Margaret

shot through the square metal tunnel, the sound of her tippy-tapping claws faded, and then there was silence. Lil looked into the black void for a moment while around her the temperature dropped and the hair on the back of her neck began to prickle.

'She's coming,' warned Nedly.

Lil stood up, and whipped round just in time to see that Hench had got to his feet too and was standing there clutching his bloodied wrist. His mouth twisted into a smirk but when he saw the look on Lil's face his expression changed. Lil knew he could feel it too: the creeps, all around him. Or more specifically: right behind him.

Lil watched as his lips began to quiver; his face rippled and for a second his features darkened and took on grey shadows as the spirit of the dead woman walked though him, and then he fainted.

'Get back!' Nedly yelled, rushing forward. Lil circled round, took a running jump at the armchair and sprang over the back of it. She crouched down low and shot a look round the side. In the centre of the room Nedly appeared to be grappling with thin air. Lil saw his sweatshirt stretch out like it was being clawed at. Inch was pulling him towards her.

'Don't let her get hold of you!' Lil yelled.

She thought she saw a fleeting look cross Nedly's face along the lines of *Thanks, I hadn't thought of that*, and then he began to shake out his right arm and Lil saw that instead of just one finger, his whole hand was glowing now; Nedly himself had dimmed but he was channelling his power into one part of his body, focusing it where it counted.

'Go on, Nedly!' she shouted.

Nedly nodded, kept his chin down, drew back his fist and released it like he was loosing an arrow. All his spectral energy was behind the punch as he twisted mid-air, spun 360 degrees with the force of his own momentum – and then fell flat on his face. He lay there motionless.

Lil raced out from behind the chair. 'Nedly!

Are you OK?' She felt the temperature in the room thaw. 'Has Inch gone?'

'Yep.' Nedly still wasn't moving.

'Margaret must have got the poppet back to Mum and Abe so they could destroy it in the furnace,' Lil explained helpfully.

'Looks that way.' Nedly pushed himself up onto his knees and from there onto his feet.

'It was shaping up to be a really impressive punch, though. Maybe even a knockout.'

He gave her a bashful shrug and blew on his knuckles. 'I've been practising that one.'

The strong sense of menace in the room had seeped away with the demise of Inch. There was only Hench to deal with now, and he was still out cold. Lil raised her eyebrows hopefully. 'That's all of the poppets gone now, right?'

Nedly's expression turned grave. 'There's still one missing. We haven't got Mr Grip yet.'

Lil flicked on her torch and ran back to the cabinet where the other poppets had been. The shelf was empty. She checked the floor, the drawers and the cupboards next door, but she couldn't find Mr Grip's poppet anywhere.

Slowly she returned to the back room, her eyes narrowed, jaw set. She nodded at the collapsed heap of Hench. 'I'll bet he knows.'

Gingerly she prodded his chest. Hench's shirt was tight and wrinkled with sweat. She pushed it again and then gave his shoulder a shake. 'Wake up!' she told him sharply and gave his nose a good pinch.

Hench sparked to life with a gasp, his eyes wide with panic. 'Get away from me!' he wheezed.

Lil looked down at him with contempt. 'Give it up, Hench. Inch is gone. They're all gone. And you're going back to jail.'

He shook his head stubbornly. 'That's what you think. This place is still haunted, all right. I can feel it.'

Lil slid her gaze towards Nedly and gave him a nod that meant *give us some space, will you?*

Nedly politely stepped back.

Hench was mumbling to himself, twisting his handkerchief into knots in his clammy hands.

'Old Henchie has just about had enough of spooks. He didn't sign up for being the one who got scared,' he whimpered.

Lil took a step closer until she was standing over him and turned the laser-like Penetrating Squint on him at close range. 'I think you want this to end just as much as we do, but you don't know how to end it.' Hench peered curiously up at Lil, and a flicker of something crossed his face. Lil let the Squint soften. 'So why don't you just hand over whichever poppets are still in the game to me and I'll take care of them?'

Hench balled the handkerchief up in his palm and kneaded it until his knuckles turned white, and then he made his choice. 'Mr Grip. He's the one you're looking for, am I right?' His hand twitched in a suggestion of the jab that he hadn't the heart to deliver, even as a mime.

Lil nodded.

'All right,' Hench agreed. Lil noticed that some of the shine had returned to his small blue eyes. 'Let's do a deal – I give you the last spook and I walk.'

Lil and Nedly exchanged glances. *So Grip was the last of them; that confirmed it.* Lil wanted to snap the deal up straight away. She wanted to put an end to this for good. She said, 'I want the key to the furnace room too.'

Hench smiled. 'Naturally.'

'OK, deal. So, where is he?'

Hench pulled himself up on one of the shelves and limped over to an old tea chest. He took off the boxes that were stacked on top and then picked up a claw hammer from the workbench and used it to crowbar the lid open.

Lil looked nervously at Nedly but tried to keep her voice steady. 'Can you give us the key to the basement first?'

But Hench wasn't listening. He was reaching deep into the tea chest, and then he pulled out the poppet.

'Careful!' Lil warned him. 'Don't wake him up!'

'Get them!' Hench threw the poppet up in a high curve. Its black bead eyes glinted as it flipped in the air and then began its descent towards Lil, the tinkle of its topknot bell ringing out in the silence.

Lil watched it plummet towards her in slow motion.

'Lil!' Nedly was shouting. 'He's getting away!'

Lil switched her attention to Hench, to see him stumbling across the workroom, dragging a sheet of bear fur that got hooked over his leg behind him. He hurled himself through the front door, into the black night and the snow, and ran.

'The key!!!' Lil yelled after him.

She and Nedly watched Hench stagger into the middle of the road, then, like a bowling pin, he was suddenly knocked off his feet and fell face down onto the frozen ground. He got up on to his knees and then, under the cold glare of the moon, they saw his eyes widen and start to bulge. He clutched at his heart and then crumpled forward, his black oily hair turning perfectly white, like a fire had spread over his skull and turned it to ash.

Chapter 26

Mr Grip

'Mr Grip,' Nedly breathed.

Very slowly they stepped backwards, through the scattered toys, past the broken jars until they hit the the workbench. From there Lil ducked round the shelves and then ran quickly down the stairs to the door to the furnace room and rapped urgently on it.

'Mum?' she whispered as loudly as she dared.

'Lil! Naomi gasped. 'What are you doing still

there? Are you OK? Is that man still here? Why aren't you?'

'Shhhh!' whispered Lil. 'Tell Abe that Mr Grip is about so you need to be really quiet, OK? Or he'll come down here after you.'

'Who's Mr –' Naomi started to ask but Lil interrupted her.

'You don't know him. Abe will explain. Trust me. Just don't make a sound. Please.'

'I –' Naomi started and then she stopped and was silent. Finally she whispered, 'Be careful.'

Lil held her hand against the door for a moment and then crept back up to the workshop where Nedly was standing by the shelves, his eyes still fixed on the road. Lil whispered as quietly as she could manage, 'What's he doing?'

Nedly shrugged and whispered back, 'He's just standing there in the snow, looking at the stars. Or a really tall building. Maybe he's waiting for an instruction?'

They both looked down at Mr Grip's poppet, which was now lying on the floor staring up at the ceiling with its crazed bead eyes and expressionless mouth. Lil tucked her hair behind her ears in a way that meant business. 'Nedly, I'm going to go for the poppet, real slow.'

Nedly looked panicked for a second but Lil continued. 'I think that might be our only shot. Agreed?' He nodded reluctantly. 'All right then.'

Trying to stay as small and quiet as possible, she crept out into the workshop, rolling her feet across the boards so they didn't creak. She reached the poppet and bent down, taking hold of the little bell between her finger and thumb, and very slowly lifted it off the ground by its topknot. She held it dangling at arm's length, like a bewitched and filthy sock, then carefully started to retrace her steps backwards to the shelves.

Then she froze. Underfoot was something soft, something that had gasped when she trod on it. Lil knew with a terrible sense of foreboding what it was – she remembered seeing it there; she used to have one herself. Froggy the Gremlin, a smiling rubber frog in a dinner suit with a squeaker in its belly. Trapped where she stood, Lil tried in vain to lift her foot slowly from the toy without letting the squeak out too, but there it was, a tiny whining cry that cut through the air like a siren.

Lil cut her losses, shot back to the shelves as quickly as possible, and joined Nedly by the paint pots.

'He heard you!'

Lil puffed out her cheeks. 'I didn't squeak him on purpose!'

Neither of them took their eyes off the empty black doorway, but only Nedly could see what stepped into it.

'He's here.'

Lil's pulse started hammering her throat. 'It's OK,' she said, gulping. 'I've got the poppet.' She gave it a quick shake and the bell sounded through the silence, sharp as a knife blade. 'Grip,' she said in her firmest voice. 'Get back to bed.'

She gave Nedly a sideways glance but he just shrugged fearfully. 'Do you hear me?' She shook the poppet again, more viciously this time. Its horrible head lolled about on its shoulders as the little bell tolled. 'Go to sleep!' Lil shouted.

The front door slammed shut and then opened supernaturally fast and then slammed again over and over. Its glass window cracked and then it smashed and the shop bell tolled like a maniacal alarm. On the sixth time the door stayed open.

Lil hunkered down behind the bench. Nedly joined her.

'Why isn't it working?' She glared at the bead-eyed poppet, at its horrible straight slash of a mouth, and then shook it again.

'Something's changed.' Nedly peered round the side of the workbench at the ghoul in the workshop and then he looked back at the poppet in Lil's hands and turned as white as a sheet. 'It's the poppet,' he whispered. 'It's not controlling him any more. He's free.'

It took Lil a minute to fully understand. 'But . . . but if he's not bound to the poppet, then how do we stop him?'

Nedly blinked at her. 'I don't think we can.'

Without warning the workbench shot away from them and then came back at triple speed. Lil folded her arms over her head, braced for impact but Nedly managed to flip it at the last minute so instead it came at them legs first, creating a shield for them to cower behind.

It was just in time. Grip began firing all he could at them; spectral winds whipped around carrying everything that had once been on the walls and pelting them with it, but the bench held strong.

The banging from downstairs started up again and went on and on, growing faster like a racing heartbeat, and joining it were shouts and yells. Lil's heart swelled at the sound. She knew that her mum and Abe were trying to draw Mr Grip away from her, to divert his attention. But it was too late for that.

The workbench strained away from them, juddering, but Nedly held it fast, his hands glowing fiercely, fingers splayed and trembling with the effort. Lil yelped as a cuddly teddy bear clambered over the wooden barricade, its features twisted into an angry scowl. She grabbed it by the paw and hurled it back over.

'Why doesn't he come nearer?'

'I . . . I suppose . . . if he's not bound to his poppet any more, then he's vulnerable. He can't be called back. If . . . if anything happens to him, that's it.' Nedly was thinking hard, still holding the bench. 'He needs to be sure he can win.'

Lil's eyes widened. 'So, if you beat him, that's it – he's finished.' She ducked out of the way of a china doll as it hurtled past.

A volley of miniature cars rained down on them like metal hailstones. Lil grabbed the lid from one of the nearby bins and held it over her head like an umbrella without a handle. 'Listen, he's not stronger than you, Nedly. He thinks he's all-powerful because he frightens people to death, but I'm not scared of him, and neither are you.'

Nedly's eyes gaped, wide and dark as manholes. 'But I am.'

'No, you're not. He's nothing. You're a hero – you saved Abe from the fire, remember; you squished this guy into a ball last time. You can beat him. I know you can.'

'Can I?' He gulped uncertainly and then hardened his eyes as he added, 'I'll try.'

Lil's leg had started shaking. 'Even if we wanted to, have we got time to run?'

'No.'

'Anyway, we can't; we couldn't leave Mum and Abe.'

'I won't leave them,' Nedly assured her. 'I won't let him past.'

He stood up and stepped forward through the bench, his slight figure burning brightly. He called back over his shoulder: 'If you get the chance to get away – take it.'

'I'm not leaving without you.'

'You have to. It's too late for me,' Nedly yelled over the crashing and shouting from downstairs and the debris flying through the air.

'Don't!' Lil yelled back at him. 'Don't ever say that.'

He looked back at her again and grinned sadly as the debris rained through him. 'But it is. I'm already dead, remember.'

Lil squinted through the storm of sawdust and bear stuffing. She saw Nedly walk forward. As he moved he shook down his arms, like he was trying to get loose of something, and his hands started to glow more fiercely, the light growing until they sparked and shone like he was holding on to flares. He held them up in front of him, chin down, head low.

The image of Grip from the newspaper flashed uninvited before Lil's eyes: the black hair dragged forward into a blunt short fringe, the flat lifeless eyes, the thin slash of a mouth. Sweat made her shiver. Peligan City's most notorious serial killer going hand to hand with an eleven-year-old boy.

Nedly pulled his fists back and Lil saw him punch at something, one fist after the other, landing blow after blow and then one, an uppercut, hit the spot because the spectral wind dropped for a second and the toys that were held in it fell to the floor.

Nedly ran forward, his face screwed up and determined. He jumped, but hit something

341

mid-air, as if an invisible brick wall had sprung up when he was already in flight. Lil watched him slide down it and crumple. Stunned and shaking his head, he scrambled backwards.

He'd almost made it to the workbench when he was yanked back and skidded across the floor, being dragged by something that suddenly whipped him into the air and shook him violently, and then it hurled him so fast and hard against the wall of shelves that all the jars on it exploded, raining glass, paintbrushes and dolls' eyes all over Lil.

Nedly lay there, balled up on the ground beside her, while all around ice grew on the plastic hair of the dolls, frosting the fur on the teddy bears and stiffening the silk pyjamas of the harlequin clown. A drawer sprang open and a clutch of jack-in-the-boxes leapt out at Lil, who smashed them away with the bin lid. The banging and shouting from downstairs grew even more frantic, but it was almost drowned out by the terrible clashing of the monkey's cymbals and the low whirr of clockwork limbs as they moved back and forth. The china-faced dolls' heads all turned.

He's stronger, Lil realised, *without his poppet.*

'You can't beat him,' she yelled. 'Stay down.'

Nedly, doubled up on the floor, held his hand out to Lil. Their fingertips touched, softly like snowflakes, and even though he was crumpled up his body began to glimmer.

Then there was a crash and scraping across the boards and a toppled cabinet hit the wall opposite. Grip was having fun.

'He knows he's got us trapped,' Nedly whispered.

'Not you,' said Lil quietly. 'Just me.'

'What?'

'You should go; you're the only one who can get out. Go, and get help. He's after you; maybe if you go he'll leave.'

Nedly scrambled into a crouch beside her. 'What if he doesn't?'

'Then we're no worse off than we were.'

'No!' Nedly shook his head, panic crossing his face. 'I'm not leaving you.'

'You can't stop him. He's too strong.'

'Neither can you.'

'But you can get help.'

'Who from?'

Lil shrugged helplessly. 'You'll think of something.'

Nedly shook his head. 'Please don't ask me to go.' His eyes had teared up.

'It's OK,' Lil said. 'You did everything you could.' Nedly's body was trembling, flickering in protest, but Lil stood her ground. 'Beat it, I said.' She raised her voice into a shout, 'Go on, get out of here!'

Nedly just had time to give her a furious look, and then he vanished.

Chapter 27

The Ghost in the Machine

Lil was alone.

She pursed her lips. *Nedly hadn't abandoned her*, she told herself. *He was getting help.* She poked her head round the workbench to get a proper look at the path she would have to take to get to the door, and then recoiled quickly as a savagely hurled rubber bunny dealt her a glancing blow. The door seemed so far away. Grip wouldn't toy with her for long. As soon as he realised that Nedly had gone he *would* make his move.

She sat with her back to the workbench while a barrage of doll parts broke against it, her hair stuck to the cold sweat on her forehead. She took a deep breath and tried to slow her heartbeat down. Fear was getting the better of her, stopping her from thinking straight. She tried so hard to swallow it. She wrapped her fingers round the pencil stub in her mac pocket and gripped it tightly. She had to make a run for it. With her free hand trembling uncontrollably, she picked up the bin lid again and held it against her shoulder.

The workbench juddered violently like a pressure cooker about to blow. Suddenly it skidded away across the floor, pivoting on one leg as it smashed against the adjacent wall, leaving Lil with only the bin lid for cover.

So this was it. Mr Grip knew she was alone. The game was over. Sick with dread, Lil drew herself up to her full height. Chills rippled her skin. Her heart was hammering in her chest.

The toys stopped clattering their hands and spinning their heads and all turned to look at her while the spectral wind, carrying dust and wood shavings, whipped at her hair, blinding her as she took one step forward.

An almost life-sized doll with long plaits and a tam o'shanter burst out of a cupboard and marched towards Lil, stiff arms and legs, lifeless eyes and lips in a pout.

Lil gripped the pencil in her fist tightly and took another step towards the door and then another. There was a huge crash from the basement.

The temperature was dropping again and the room was emptied of any remaining warmth. Lil could feel it being sucked away.

'Nedly, where are you?' she whispered. The pencil in her fist snapped, she felt the unmistakable touch of freezer burn on her throat and then, shockingly, a sweaty hand grabbed hers and swung her back. And there was her mother, standing in front of her, just as the tam o'shanter doll threw itself at Lil. Naomi swerved to block it and the doll's hard plastic feet caught her above one eye, smashing the lens of her spectacles.

'Ow!' she yelped, using her sleeve to wipe away the blood that trickled down 'Where did that come from?'

Margaret skittered in and Abe staggered behind her. He was covered in crumbled plaster like a flour-dusted ogre, his reddened eyes blinking and chest heaving.

Naomi squinted into the dark and dusty air. 'Where's the goon?' Lil felt her mother's arm tighten round her and hold on fast. With her other hand Naomi rootled around blindly and found the claw hammer, which she wielded like a bat.

'Out there.' Lil pointed towards the door. 'He ran away.'

'Good.' Naomi nodded frantically for a second and then said, 'What about the other one, Grip?'

Lil's breath plumed out before her as she whispered, 'He's still here.'

The air turned arctic, so cold that it hurt to breathe. A fear began in Lil's belly, growing quickly, spreading out its tentacles and wrapping itself around her bones.

Margaret glared at a spot on the other side of the room. Her back fur punked up, her ears pinned back, and her little body was shaking. Her whole face was wrinkled up with the effort of baring all her teeth at once, trying to look more frightening than frightened. Abe followed her gaze and the colour drained from his face. He could feel what he couldn't see. He laid his hand on the first thing it came to, a hard plastic doll with a shock of sandy curls, and brandished it.

Lil flashed a sideways glance at him.

'I just feel better with something in my hand,' he muttered. 'Where's the kid?'

'Gone to get help. I told him to.'

Abe frowned at her in disbelief. 'So what do we do now?'

'What do we do about what?' Naomi looked askance at them. 'There's nobody here but us.'

Lil couldn't make her mouth speak, the words got trapped somewhere in her throat. She pointed, following Margaret's stare.

'Is he hiding?' Naomi asked. She let go of Lil's hand.

'Naomi, wait! No!' Abe tried to grab for her, to pull her out of Grip's reach but Naomi was already striding ahead. Suddenly she stopped and raised her hand to her throat as panic and confusion hit her face.

'NOOOOOO!' Abe roared as he leapt forward.

There was a blinding light, glass smashing and wood splintering as something huge crashed through the front entrance, annihilating the door and most of the shop window.

Powerful magnesium headlights cut through the clouds of dust. The glass from the shattered window twinkled sharply. For a moment the only sound was the ticking of a cooling engine and then the zip of a sliding metal door.

Three figures in white hazmat jumpsuits with helmets that looked like welders' masks emerged cautiously and began crunching their way over the broken toys, trampling plastic heads underfoot. The headlights glanced off their reflective orange visors as they passed in front of Abe, Lil and Naomi, who were frozen in surprise. Margaret fled to her safe place by Abe's shoes and sat on one of them.

The jumpsuited figures stood in a line at what used to be the front of the shop. In their gloved hands they held what looked like consoles with roaming antennae.

Lil saw the few remaining dolls on the shelves glance sideways to watch them.

'Watch out!' she shouted, but the jumpsuits' feet were firmly planted, their fingers engaged with pressing buttons on the consoles – all except the middle suit, who held up a single finger as if to say 'Watch this!'

They flicked a switch and a net of green luminous laser light appeared, covering the whole room in a shimmering grid. Lil, Abe and Naomi all backed away as far as possible from the green rays that flared as they reached eye level.

The finger went up again, the angle of it seeming to suggest 'Don't move!', and they froze. The grid flickered over surfaces, casting the room in an eerie green light.

'What's happening?' hissed Lil.

'Beats me,' replied Abe.

Naomi still seemed to be in shock.

They stared at the grid, hypnotised by the lines that sliced through the air. Lil squinted as she tried to focus on one area where the lines were broken, a dark shadow on the grid. The light blinked over the object it had located. Something man-shaped.

Grip! thought Lil. *They can see him.*

There was some excitable elbowing going on and then the middle jumpsuit stepped forward. The dark man-shaped mass was moving ahead, blocking out the gridlines, rippling through as it passed them.

The jumpsuit twisted a dial and the squares on the grid got smaller, the matrix contracted, focusing on the area where Grip was. The hum increased, the grid tightened and Grip's movement became more erratic, thrashing as if trapped.

The jumpsuit ratcheted it up a notch. Abe picked up Margaret and he, Lil and Naomi retreated as far as they could as the three figures moved forward as one, their net tightening. There was a high-pitched whine, like an electrical tone, and Margaret howled along to it. The whine got louder, the grids got smaller and then another noise joined the whine, an echoing cry of rage. Then – *zoowp!* Like a net being reverse-sprung, Grip, the grid, everything, was sucked back into the box and there was silence.

Nobody moved.

The ambient temperature rose a few degrees. The jumpsuit with the box inspected it carefully; it was leaking a thin black smoke, which smelt of sugar puffs and ammonia. After a few moments they gave a stiff nod of their bulbous glass-fronted heads and the tension seemed to snap like an old rubber band.

One of the other suits yelled, 'Whooop!' and

the third replied with an even louder 'Whooo-hoooop!' and threw a punch at the air. One gave a clumsy attempt at giving the others a high-five, and then a three-way hug that involved lots of awkward back slapping.

Finally a jumpsuit took the box and disappeared with it into the back of the van. Then the other two began picking up material from the floor and stuffing it into hazardous waste bags and scanning it all with a device that looked like a hair-dryer, while the third reappeared and sprayed some kind of gas out of a canister over any toys that were still on the shelves.

Lil, Naomi, Abe and Margaret still stood there, unmoving in the dust and rubble. No one spoke to them. It was as though, at least as far as the jumpsuits were concerned, they weren't really there.

Naomi recovered at last. 'We should go,' she whispered. 'Before they start asking us awkward questions.' She nodded to the exit.

Where the door and window had once been there was now just a lot of broken glass, shattered wood and the van the jumpsuits had arrived in. As they edged their way towards it one of the jumpsuits put out a hand to indicate that they should stop. Lil could hear the hiss of radio static as he communicated with one of the others, and then the jumpsuit with the hair-dryer device came over and passed it over each of their bodies.

He scanned them with no more interest than he had anything else. The only time he hesitated was with Lil, when he ran the scanner over her twice, and then reached out a scientific finger and prodded her on the forehead with it, before tapping the machine against his gloved palm to fix whatever problem had caused the rogue reading. Then he moved on, following some wave of activity elsewhere.

Another jumpsuit approached, unclipped their helmet and pulled off the hood beneath, revealing a sharp-featured woman with flushed cheeks and strong eyebrows. Strands of her long grey hair were plastered sweatily against her neck.

'Are you all right?' she asked them.

The three nodded mutely.

Then Lil started to explain, 'There's a man outside, in the snow –'

But the woman cut her off. 'That's not our responsibility. You need to clear the area.'

Lil, Abe and Naomi exchanged confused glances. Then one of the team come over, his orange visor reflecting the woman's face back at her, and reported in his nasal radio voice: 'We've picked up another reading, Virgil.'

The woman called Virgil gave him a curt nod. 'We're not done here yet.' She replaced her own helmet. The next time she spoke it was in a tinny radio voice. 'Exit at the front. Stay away from the van,' she warned, and then turned and strode off.

Abe put Margaret down and she trotted purposefully to the pile of broken doll parts that were banked up against the shelves and started digging, burrowing down until she found what she was looking for: the bead-eyed poppet. She nipped hold of it with her little front teeth, carried it over to where Lil stood and dutifully sat down.

'Good idea,' said Lil. 'Just in case.' She took hold of the creepy poppet with her fingers over the bell to keep it from ringing out.

'I've just got to take care of something,' she whispered to Abe and took two steps backwards, into the darkness, away through the back room and down the stairs. She climbed through the smashed-in doorway, picking her way past broken plasterboard, and finally walking over the fallen door like a drawbridge.

Once inside, she opened the furnace and threw Mr Grip's poppet into the flames. Its sack-cloth body ignited instantly; light burst briefly in its chest as the flammable stuffing went up, the thread mouth curled to ash and the plastic bead eyes melted into slick black tears. Within seconds it was no more than a topknot and a white-hot bell.

Chapter 28

An Early Breakfast

They stumbled over the collapsed shopfront and out into the snow.

Lil pulled her notebook out of her back pocket as they squeezed past what turned out to be a silver transit van and paused to scribble down the lettering on the side, which read 'Ghostcatcher Inc'.

Naomi nodded at it. 'Gordian said she had a plan to deal with the so-called hauntings. I guess they are it.'

Abe, who had to do more squeezing than the others, was the last to emerge onto the street. He nodded at the van and said 'Big news!' in a voice that was short on breath.

Naomi agreed. 'Whatever this is, it's going to make some story.' She turned to Lil, who felt her heart lifting for a moment at the thought of working with her mother on the scoop. 'Where's the nearest phone box?'

Lil's heart sank again. Reluctantly she pointed down Bead Street. 'About a block that way. Can I come too?'

Naomi gave her a rueful look. 'Not this time. Wait for me at the Picture House.' She turned to go.

'Mum?' Lil slipped her rucksack off her shoulders and rummaged around inside. She pulled out her report on the Cornelius Gallows/ Alector Lankin situation and offered it up. 'You better take this too. Gallows is behind all this and someone better break the story about him being holed up in the prison before he escapes again.'

Naomi took hold of the papers and Lil let them go.

As she jogged away down the road, Abe gave Lil a grim smile. 'Sorry we got separated back there, kiddo.'

Lil shrugged. 'It's OK. I wasn't alone.'

'You two did all right.' He looked meaningfully at a bit of empty space by Lil.

'It's just me here,' she said. 'But, yeah, we did OK, until Mr Grip showed up. Thanks for sending Margaret by the way; she was a big help.'

'That was your mother's idea.'

'I'll bet,' said Lil. 'I better go and find Nedly.' She indicated the alleyway that ran alongside the doll hospital. 'Catch up with you in a minute.'

Lil slowly made her way towards the back of the building, running her hand along the brickwork, trying to find a spot that was colder than the rest, where Nedly had passed through, or was hiding. 'Nedly, are you in there?' she whispered every couple of feet.

She was just past the bins when a small voice

replied, 'I'm here.' He was leaning against the opposite wall, almost invisible in the darkness.

'Phew!' said Lil. 'You're OK.' She studied him for a moment; he was flickering slightly. '*Are you OK?*'

Nedly shrugged. 'I'm just glad you got out of there all right. I wasn't sure . . .' They heard a noise from beyond the wall, someone pushing aside toppled shelving units by the sound of it. 'Ghostcatcher?' Nedly peered up the alley where the rear of the van could be seen – its lights illuminating the surrounding snow.

Lil nodded enthusiastically. 'You should have seen the laser thing they netted Grip with. It was a-mazing. I'm not sure what it did exactly but it looked really cool. He didn't stand a chance; it was all over in a few seconds. They just got him fixed in this, like, cage of green light and then – *squerp!* Sucked him out of the room!' Nedly's already pale face turned paler and he shuddered. 'But I torched his poppet anyway,' Lil assured him. 'Just in case.'

They headed off out of the alleyway and

around the corner towards the cinema. Lil lowered her voice as they neared the bricked-up fire exit at the back of the doll hospital.

She pointed at the man sleeping soundly in the doorway, in the pitch that had once belonged to Delilah. 'I can't believe he slept through all that.'

'What makes you think I'm asleep?' His voice cut through the air. 'The dead themselves couldn't rest with that racket going on in there.'

It took Lil a moment to get over the start he'd given her. 'Sorry. But you had your eyes closed again so . . .'

'I can close my eyes whenever I like,' he fired back. 'You can thank your stars I was awake. Who do you think called the number?'

'What number?'

He rummaged in a bag filled with old newspapers, pulled out a leaflet and held it out to her. It was the Haunting Hotline flyer.

Lil stared at it in disbelief. 'This thing is real?'

'You're holding it, aren't you?' The man

snatched the flyer back out of her hands. 'I figured you all needed some help in there; you were making enough noise about it.'

Lil tried to smile at him through her gritted teeth. 'OK, well, thanks, I suppose.'

'You suppose right,' he huffed back, and then with a shake of his head he pulled his sleeping bag up over his shoulder and hunkered down into his cardboard nest.

'You asked me to go for help.' Nedly grimaced. 'He was it.'

They crossed the road at the corner, and as soon as they were out of earshot Lil said, 'Where did you find the flyer?'

'They're everywhere,' he told her. 'Someone must have dropped a load over the city while we were in the doll hospital. I had to blow it at him a few times and put the frighteners on him a bit before he sat up and took notice, but eventually he got the message.'

'You did all right, Nedly.' She looked serious for a moment, thinking how she had never really believed that he would leave her and how scared she had been when he did. In the end she just said, 'I knew you would think of something.'

Abe and Margaret had taken shelter under the marquee of the Limelight Picture House while they waited for the Potkins to catch up. Lil and Nedly joined them, sitting in a row along the top step where the snow was held off by the awning.

Abe took off his hat and tapped the rubble out of the crease. Margaret left his side and trotted round to where Nedly was sitting. She didn't exactly sit next to him, but she was voluntarily closer than she had ever been.

'Oh, it's like that, is it?' Abe sighed at the inevitability of it all, sank back onto the pavement and buried his chin in his collar.

Lil winked at Nedly. 'Looks like you've got company.'

'You did a great job in there, Margaret.' Nedly reached out a hand to stroke her but she growled and he retracted it. Then the little dog wrinkled her forehead and peeled back her lips. It was a mixed-up expression, but not unlike a smile.

'That's a pretty creepy face, Margaret,' Lil said, but Nedly was grinning.

Nobody spoke for a while after that. Lil was tired and her eyes were watering with the plaster dust she had rubbed into them. She wiped the tears away, leaving her cheeks slightly cleaner than the rest of her face.

Naomi waved as she rounded the corner, the streetlight throwing her shadow out across the snow as if she were a giant.

Abe replaced the slightly cleaner hat on his dusty head and called out to her. 'That didn't take long.'

'I put a call in to the office. Quake is on her way. I left the file for her.' Naomi climbed the steps up to where they were sitting.

Lil kept her eyes on her boots. 'Aren't you going back to the scene for the scoop?'

'Nah, I've got better things to do tonight.' She sat down beside Lil who glanced across and noticed the thin trickle of blood running down the bridge of her mother's nose and her cracked glasses.

'Are you all right, Mum?'

Naomi gingerly touched two fingers to the cut. 'Some doll kicked me in the head, but I'll live.' She paused to give Lil a look-over too. 'How about you? Are you OK?'

Lil nodded shakily.

'What about the other kid? The one who went for help. Are they still around?'

'He's here somewhere.' Lil looked across at Nedly and her eye flickered in a wink.

'Well, the cavalry, or whatever that was, arrived just in time, so I'd like to thank him.'

'I'll let him know, if I see him.'

'You should have gone to get help too, you know?'

Lil dug her boot into the snow and forged a crescent. 'I didn't want to leave you down there. Anyway, the goon was in the way; one of us had to distract him.'

'Well, it was stupid and brave to stick around.'

Lil snorted off the half-compliment. 'It's fair to say I was petrified the whole time.' She thought for a moment and then added, 'Weren't *you*?'

Naomi nodded. 'More scared than I've ever been in my life. You were up there, and I was trapped in the cellar. I couldn't see how to get to you . . .'

Lil gave her a lopsided smile. 'You completely destroyed that door.'

Naomi smiled back. 'Abe helped.'

They sat in silence for a minute or two and then Lil tried again. 'I meant in the workshop. Weren't you scared then?'

'You mean of the ghost?' Naomi crooked her fingers around the word 'ghost' in a that-made-up-thing-that-isn't-real way. 'The laser show was good but sure as eggs are eggs I didn't see anything I would call supernatural.'

Lil looked past her mother at Nedly. He was talking animatedly to Margaret, saying, 'I know you weren't keen on the ball but I've been thinking maybe I got that wrong, maybe you're more of a stick dog. I can do that – I'll just need a bit of practice. And a stick.'

Naomi tilted her head to catch Lil's eye again and then reached out to tuck a lock of hair behind her ear. 'I know I don't say it often, but I am proud of you, kiddo.'

Lil couldn't stop the reflex shrug that came whenever anyone said something that she had no reply for, but then she bit her lip and managed to whisper, almost loud enough for Naomi to hear, 'I'm proud of you too, Mum.'

It had been a long night. Behind the street lamps the sky was still as black as pitch, but Lil suddenly had the hopeful feeling that somewhere in the world the sun was rising.

'So,' she said, 'what now?'

Naomi levered herself onto her feet and held out a hand. 'How about an early breakfast?'

Lil looked at her watch. 'It's twenty past midnight.'

'I know. But I bet I can get the Nite Jar to reopen.'

Abe made a show of brushing the snow off his trousers to avoid looking at anyone. 'Well, I'll be seeing you.'

Lil was taken aback. 'Aren't you coming?'

'No,' Abe said gruffly. 'I've got some stuff to

do, and I have to be somewhere else to do it.'

'It's the middle of the night,' said Lil. 'Where else would you need to be?'

'Asleep. In bed.' He softened slightly and shrugged. 'You don't really want me there. Anyway, I'm all dusty and covered in bear fur.'

Naomi hooked her own plaster-caked arm, which was sprinkled with sawdust and even some blood from a particularly bad splinter, through his. 'So am I.'

'Yeah, well, it suits you,' said Abe, with a bashful smile. 'All right then, I'm in, if you're buying.' Together they strolled off down Spooner Row towards the Nite Jar with Margaret trotting solemnly at their heels.

Nedly glanced back towards the alley where the Ghostcatcher van was parked. 'You know, for a minute there I thought they were going to come after me too.'

'Yeah,' admitted Lil. 'Even their high-tech equipment might not be able to tell the difference between the good guys and the bad guys.'

Nedly's eyes darkened. Leaflets for the Haunting Hotline were scattered all about, lying on the wet ground, their red lettering streaking the snow like blood spots. A chilling breeze circled the road at the corner and blew the snow straight through him. 'I better keep out of their way then,' he murmured to himself.

Lil smiled at Nedly and said, 'So, what do you want to do now?'

He wrinkled his nose thoughtfully. 'When we get to the cafe, will you order an extra sausage for me? I . . . I was going to give it to Margaret.'

Lil grinned at him. 'She'd like that, but I meant now that we've scuppered Gallows' plan and destroyed all his poppets, what do you want to do now?' The snow had started falling again, silently muddling the air and covering Lil's footprints along the path. 'Me and you together, I reckon we could do anything.'

Nedly grinned back at her, his eyes shining in the pearly glow of the streetlights. 'Sounds good to me.'

Acknowledgements

A huge thank-you to: Emma Matthewson and Jenny Jacoby, Nick Stearn, Jeff Jamieson, Tina Mories and everyone at Piccadilly Press who has worked on *Potkin and Stubbs* with such passion behind the scenes.

Fellow writers Ruth Dugdall, Jane Bailey, Morag Liffen and Liz Ferretti for the workshopping, Nick Smith for the website and Graham Felce for the photography; Amanda and Neil Davidson for showing me the bright lights of the big city; Catherine Larner for all sorts of book-related advice and support, and David Schmid for an excellent online course on mystery writing and suspense.

Finally, to my family and my friends – sorry you didn't see me very much, but thanks for the space and time, and for still being there when I resurfaced.

Sophie Green

Sophie Green writes children's fiction, short stories and scripts. She has a degree in zoology and an interest in folklore. She was born in Suffolk, where she works as a children's librarian for the public library service.

Karl James Mountford

Karl James Mountford was born in Germany and is now a full-time illustrator based in Wales.

He studied illustration at Swansea College of Art and was also the artist in residence there while studying for his M.A. in Visual Communication.

He now spends most of his day illustrating all types of awesome stories and genres.

Piccadilly
P R E S S

Thank you for choosing a Piccadilly Press book.

If you would like to know more about our
authors, our books or if you'd just like to know
what we're up to, you can find us online.

www.piccadillypress.co.uk

And you can also find us on:

We hope to see you soon!